ENCOUNTER À LA BUTCHER

The Butcher's open-handed slap spun the car attendant completely around and flung him to the floor. Before he could recover and scramble to his feet, the Butcher gathered a big handful of shirt and necktie up close to Hugues's throat and held him on his knees.

"You know who I am, son of a bitch?"

Hugues blanched, and neighed in abject terror.

In a deft movement Butcher plucked out the switchblade that was sheathed to his left ankle. As the seven and one-half inches of razor-sharp steel flashed into view only inches from his throat, Hugues's eyeballs bulged out of their sockets.

Butcher snarled savagely as he pressed the back edge of the switchblade against the attendant's jugular vein.

"Either you talk and talk loud and fast, or else you get butchered. Which will it be?"

The Butcher Series

And more to come . . .

THE BUTCHER
KILLER'S CARGO

by
Stuart Jason

PINNACLE BOOKS • NEW YORK CITY

THE BUTCHER: KILLER'S CARGO

An original Pinnacle Books edition, published for the
first time anywhere.

ISBN: 0-523-00429-X

First printing, September 1974

Printed in the United States of America

PINNACLE BOOKS, INC.
275 Madison Avenue
New York, N.Y. 10016

KILLER'S CARGO

PROLOGUE

"Whadda ya mean quit?" the other crime overlords had snarled in angry alarm. *"You can't quit! Ain't nobody quits the Syndicate and lives! You know that! What's wrong with you all of a sudden anyway? You gone nuts or something? You got the whole East Coast Division sewed up tighter'n a drum: girly houses, wire services, racetracks, the numbers, everything—and you wanna quit? Huh-uh! Quit and how long you think you're gonna live, huh? A day? Two days? A week if you're lucky? Huh-uh! You don't quit the Syndicate! Not never! You're the toughest, meanest son of a bitch we ever seen operate, and you pack the fastest heater since Dillinger came down the pike, but quit the Syndicate and you're dead! Make book on it!"*

Yet he had quit, anyway. Simply walked out and never gone back. At the apex of the underworld success ladder, when his private coffers were constantly filled to overflowing, and numerous Swiss bank accounts held more money than any man could spend, he had turned his back and walked away. And from that day forward Bucher's life became a pressure-cooker existence, at times reminding him of a blood-and-guts Hollywood B-grade extravaganza produced over the weekend on a shoe string. For the day he

1

walked out on the Syndicate his former business associates quietly placed a hundred-thousand-dollar, dead-only price tag on his head. Moreover, when his trail became strewn with the bodies of eager-beaver gunsels who had tried to collect, interest in the reward flagged even among the Syndicate's most blood-lustful killers. So, in order to revive the interest, the Syndicate had upped the hit price to a quarter of a million dollars.

Who is this Bucher, this man with only a one-word name, a name the underworld had bastardized into the Butcher?

It all began one wintry day years ago at St. Joseph's Orphanage in Knoxville, Tennessee, when the chief custodian, the Reverend Mr. Isham Green, discovered the blanket-wrapped foundling on the orphanage doorstep. This discovery neither elated nor depressed the good man, for even at that early hour of the morning he was too far gone in his secret indulgence to feel much of anything. In short, Reverend Green was already well on his way to being so goes the saying, as drunk as a boiled owl, for he did truly love the bottle—providing said bottle contained an alcoholic beverage and was within arm's reach.

Even so, on the credit side of the ledger it can honestly be said that the bottle was not Isham Green's only love. He also loved books, particularly those books lauding the accomplishments of history's great Christians. And these two loves were contributing factors to the choice of the newly discovered foundling's one-word name—Bucher.

It was the commendable practice of the Welfare Department to give all orphans becoming its wards a physical examination as soon as possible. This examination was performed by an incredibly ugly young doctor named Allen Adams. Adams was a very impatient man—impatient with life in general and especially impatient with drunken orphanage custodians. The examination of the foundling took place in Reverend Green's cramped, untidy office-cum-library, the infant lying on its blanket atop the reverend's desk.

Also atop the desk at the time was one of Reverend Green's favorite volumes, a collection of short biographies of history's great Christians. The volume was open at the biography of Bucher, famous sixteenth-century German Protestant and Hebraist. Therefore, when incredibly ugly, enormously impatient young Dr. Adams, filling out the birth certificate, asked: "Name?" the thoroughly intoxicated Isham Green, his misty eyes on the open book, replied: "Bucher." This name Dr. Adams hastily scrawled in the appropriate blank. And thus it was that Bucher was named Bucher and nothing else.

The manner in which Bucher became the Syndicate's most feared gun, then the dread scourge of the underworld, is quite a different story indeed, a story that began the day a ten-year-old orphan named Bucher went down to the railroad tracks not far from the orphanage, climbed into the rear of a tractor-trailer rig and went to sleep. The rig was loaded with eider down bedding slated for the mansion of a jaded millionairess playgirl in Chicago. He continued to sleep when the trailer's doors were closed and sealed by the drivers—and the next time Bucher saw the sun, it was over the Windy City.

In Chicago Bucher survived by making swift raids on sidewalk fruit and vegetable displays and by the

3

grace of garbage cans. One day he met little Luigi Orazio, and things took a decided turn for the better.

Little Luigi Orazio was Bucher's own age, and each day a special nurse brought him in a wheelchair to the playground where Bucher had come to hang out. Little Luigi was a thin, frail, emaciated child, the only son of Tino and Maria Orazio. He was dying of leukemia.

In that mysterious manner of things only children understand, Luigi adopted Bucher as his brother and took him home to meet Momma Maria and Poppa Tino. When Momma and Poppa Orazio saw the worship glowing in their little son's eyes when the scrawny, half-starved, ragged alley urchin was around, in their hearts they adopted Bucher, too.

Bucher joined the Orazio household and time passed. And with its passing little Luigi passed on to a better life. When little Luigi died, Bucher's presence eased the sorrow of the grieving parents.

It was Poppa Tino Orazio who first recognized in young Bucher two exceptionally rare and priceless talents—muscular reflexes so incredibly swift that they deceived the very eye and jungle animal survival instincts, constantly alert and so keenly tuned that they bordered precognition. To Tino Orazio, a graduate of Chicago's sewer-world of crime, life was at best a day-to-day struggle. Therefore he saw absolutely nothing amiss in giving young Bucher every opportunity to develop his priceless talents; they would provide the lad with the greatest assurance of survival in that dangerous and violent environment.

Now, in those post-Capone days when the ill-famed Four Deuces existed no longer as the throne room of gangland's once mighty Alphonso, when the Bloody

4

Bucket had ceased to be, the chiefs of the city-wide crime empires across the land decided it was time to consolidate. And thus it was that the nation-wide criminal organization known as the Syndicate became a fact in the American way of life. Tino Orazio, a man of considerable power and influence in Chicago's underworld, was elected to serve as the Syndicate's first chairman of the board.

By this time Bucher was already the toughest, meanest, and fastest gun organized crime had ever seen, and, in keeping with the underworld's idiosyncratic compulsion for nicknames, was already called the Butcher. On the eleventh anniversary of little Luigi Orazio's death an incident occurred, the aftermath of which proved to many that Bucher's nickname had been aptly chosen.

Bucher had chauffeured the Orazios to the cemetery to place flowers on their son's grave that day, and as they were leaving, Momma and Poppa were machine-gunned to death by four torpedoes in a speeding touring car. Bucher witnessed these murders. He also recognized the killers. And the swift and terrible vengeance he wreaked on the four—and on the others of the upstart underworld faction they represented—filled nine graves and became legend in the Windy City.

Shortly thereafter Bucher became a young man on the go, a young man whose ice-blood cunning and tiger savagery called the shots of an incredibly fast and mindless gun. He soon blazed his way, rung by bloody rung, up the corpse-strewn ladder of underworld success until he became the undisputed crime overlord of the Syndicate's powerful East Coast Division.

Then came the day when Bucher looked around

him and asked himself some questions about the means he had employed to acquire his wealth and power. When the answers to these questions came to him, he was sickened to the very depths of his soul. At the next meeting of the Syndicate's crime overlords he announced he was quitting the organization.

Not long after Bucher's break with the Syndicate, two neatly dressed young men from Washington located him in a Detroit hotel room.

"Mr. Bucher," said one of the young men, "with your intimate knowledge of organized crime you can be of invaluable service to your country. As a special undercover agent . . ."

They offered him a contract which he ignored, a salary, which he laughed at; yet in the end he accepted their proposition because he saw in it the opportunity of atoning, in his own mind at least, for some of his grisly past.

Before leaving, the two young men from Washington gave him a telephone number, exclusively his and never unattended, and the code name Iceman. Bucher had agreed to become a part of White Hat, a security organization so super-hush-hush no hint of its existence could ever be found in the president's fiscal reports or budget requests to Congress.

And thus it was that the ex-crime overlord of the Syndicate's East Coast Division became the dreaded scourge of the underworld.

And since becoming a member of the White Hat security organization, he had undertaken numerous difficult assignments. Yet the one he was about to begin could only be categorized as baffling. He was anxious to get more information than the brief telegram the White Hat's director provided. Yet brief or not, the case involved a matter that, with his knowledge of Syndicate operations, seemed a long way out in left field.

The telegram had referred to a tranquilizing gas. And what the hell would the Syndicate want with a tranquilizing gas? Prostitution, numbers, wire services, narcotics, racetracks, and the like all fell under the aegis of the Syndicate as he knew it. But a tranquilizing gas . . . ?

Whether the Syndicate was involved or not, he'd learn the facts as soon as he reached the airport, where White Hat's director awaited him for a conference. But before he could go to the airport, he had to take care of the two Syndicate triggermen who'd cut into his trail earlier in the evening. He was pretty sure the two were Shad McGurk and Sweets Malloy and that the cruds were salivating for the quarter-million-dollar kill-price on his head, and unless he dealt with them properly, he'd never make it to that conference.

CHAPTER ONE

A silent scream of despair erupted from the city; the reek of hate and greed and blood-lust laced the pre-dawn gloom, and the cold, remorseless hands of death crept in to search the freightyard area where the big, raw-boned man crouched among the black shadows camouflaging the warehouse doorway.

Bucher cursed in self-disgust and anger. Like a dimwit tyro gunman, he had goofed, had thought the two killers were on his trail, right behind him. And they had been. But they had circled in their station wagon through a cramped alley and opened fire from across the desolate street.

Again the deadly Tommy gun's staccato rent the hushed quiet, and heavy .45 slugs chewed in mindless rage at the wooden door above Bucher's head. A flock of splinters showered down around him, and again he cursed, but this time in relief. His sharp eyes had located the killers from the furiously blinking muzzle of the Tommy gun, and this despite the fact that the weapon was equipped with a flash-hider.

Had Bucher harbored any doubts as to the identity of his assailants, this dispelled them. Shad McGurk, whom he'd known years before, had always favored a flash-hider on his sub-Thompson; and if one of the killers was McGurk, the other was Sweets Malloy. Both had been together since the days of Murder, Inc. A chilly snarl washed across Bucher's hard face. Both gunsels were now drooling for the quarter-million in blood money on his head.

And they just might collect that blood money, Bucher cautioned himself dourly, unless he made a move in the right direction—and in a hurry. The cops would be there soon, of course, drawn by the yammer of McGurk's machine gun, but Bucher would well be dead by then. Death already permeated the damp dawn, and it took a lot less time to kill a man than to tell of it.

Once more the heavy slugs from the Tommy gun chewed into the door behind him. Just as the door gave a dull groan of shattered wood and protesting hinges, Bucher threw himself to the sidewalk and squirmed around to peer at the place where he had been crouching. The door looked as if a thousand angry woodpeckers had attacked it, venting their collective spleen, for the door now sagged loosely on one hinge, its lock broken.

Uncoiling his powerful muscles without completely rising to his feet, Bucher plunged toward the door, hit it head first, further splintering the wood, and rolled inside the building.

Since the neighborhood had appeared deserted when he had left his rented car several minutes ago, Bucher had automatically assumed that the warehouse would be deserted also. In this he was correct. But inside the building it wasn't as dark as he'd expected. Twenty yards to his left and toward the rear of the building the belligerent glow of a shaded bulb cast

9

an aggressive circle of light around a scarred and ancient desk. On the desk was a telephone.

A half-dozen heartbeats later, Bucher was at the desk and dialing the phone. The instant he dialed the last digit he cut the light, plunging the interior of the building into inky blackness. Impatiently, he waited through a short series of electronic sounds, then over the wire a low voice said:

"Go ahead."

"This is the Iceman," Bucher replied quietly. He then proceeded to give his location and a terse rundown of the situation, concluding with: "McGurk and Malloy are no problem, but McGurk has been running off at the Tommy gun, which is certain to draw the cops. I'll probably need help getting sprung." He hung up.

During this brief conversation Bucher's eyes had not left the broken door through which he had entered, and now that his eyes were adjusted to the heavier darkness inside, the outline of the doorway was clearly visible against the approaching day. Cautiously he made his way to the door, stood to one side of it, and uttered the low, gaspy groan of one mortally wounded. He waited, listening intently, straining to catch some sound from the killers. When he heard nothing, he groaned a second time, terminating this one with the enfeebled cry of: "Help me! For God's sake somebody help me!" Again he waited, listening.

At last a chortle of malicious glee reached his ears, then the words: "I told you I got the creep. I told you I got him, Sweets. Aint's nothing stands up against me and my little ol' chopper."

Bucher recognized the voice as Shad McGurk's.

"Yeahhh," Sweets Malloy oozed gooily. "And

think of them quarter of a million clams we made for a couple of hours work. *Hot-ziggity!*" Shoe leather thumped the pavement briefly as Sweets Malloy did a small clog of joy. "Come on. Let's go finish the bum off."

Hoping to further stimulate their eagerness to finish the job they thought they had under control, Bucher placed a big hand over the thin gash of his mouth and again loosed those smothered, tortured sounds of one stricken unto death.

Out on the sidewalk a dozen yards to the right of the broken door where Bucher stood concealed and waiting, a lone street lamp cast a pool of pearly light. The mouth of the alley from where the killers had opened fire was slightly beyond this light and across the street. Thus Bucher had an ideal view of the killers' line of approach, and when he saw them enter the pool of light, he stepped quickly out onto the sidewalk.

There was something catlike in the movements of this big raw-boned man whose name the Syndicate had bastardized into the Butcher, something predatory; an almost tangible aura of the savagery and impending violence one sees in a tiger stalking its kill. The two men who sought to take his life had reached the center of the pearly light when Shad McGurk recoiled as if bitten by a deadly viper.

"The Butcher!" McGurk shouted. He had a wide mouth, splayed nostrils, and very little chin or forehead. Nor was the image improved by his broad, squat body. All in all, Shad McGurk greatly resembled a toad. He stood transfixed, frozen in his tracks, as did Sweets Malloy, the muzzle of McGurk's cherished Tommy gun pointing earthward.

11

"You boys looking for someone?" Bucher snarled softly.

"Ha! Ha!" Sweets Malloy said without mirth. Malloy's cadaverous countenance and skinny frame bespoke of nothing so much as a man on the verge of starvation. He sported a .30 caliber Peacemaker equipped with a thirty-round banana clip.

"Yeah," McGurk blurted. "We thought—"

"You thought I was fatally wounded," Bucher cut in, still snarling. "McGurk, you couldn't hit the side of the Empire State Building with that typewriter of yours."

McGurk bridled threateningly. "You ain't so good with that heater of yours."

The words that rumbled from Bucher's chest had that breathy quality of restrained savagery. "Then make your bid, punks—both of you."

The words acted as a trigger. McGurk snapped the muzzle of his chopper up in Bucher's direction, an expression of unholy glee on his froggish face, and—

"Koosh!"

The thick-barreled, silencered Walther P-38 that appeared in Bucher's big hand sighed softly, its heavy 9mm slug creating a third and smaller eye squarely between McGurk's other two. The force of the slug shattered his brainpan and, in exploding out the rear of his skull, hurled the man backward and sideways off his feet, his weapon clattering to the concrete.

Sweets Malloy's death face became warped with fury and blood-lust as his bony fingers curled around the trigger of his Peacemaker. "You son of a—!"

"Koosh!"

Again came the Walther's death sigh, and Malloy's

weapon also clattered to the concrete. He lurched wildly once, then regained his balance and stood there staring down in awe at the crimson spreading across the front of his cashmere blazer. A keen hiss resembling the sound of air brakes issued from his scrawny lips, and he collapsed and died without issuing another sound.

Bucher leathered his piece, swearing absently in disgust, the bitter-sour taste of defeat in his mouth. He turned in the direction of the car he had rented to go to the airport for a conference with White Hat's director when the police patrol car came screeching to a halt beside him.

Bucher stood in front of the desk of Homicide Captain Mack Whetson, who sat opposite him, glowering up at him in open belligerence. On the desk between them lay the things the arresting officers had taken off Bucher during their search: a switchblade knife they had found sheathed to his left ankle, a pair of brass knucks, a money belt containing approximately twenty thousand dollars, and the silencered Walther. Captain Whetson looked down at the single sheet of paper in Bucher's "make" folder and read for the fifth time:

"Bucher is thirty-seven years old, six feet three inches tall, and weighs one hundred ninety pounds stripped. At one time he was crime overlord of the Syndicate's East Coast Division, but for a reason yet unknown he quit the Syndicate some time ago. In retaliation for this, the underworld now has a $250,000 'dead-only' reward on his head. Bucher is believed to have several Swiss bank accounts and is to be considered extremely dangerous when crossed or cornered."

"Crap!" Captain Whetson spat in his very best criminal-intimidating tone. "You don't look 'extremely dangerous' to me!"

To this Bucher said nothing, his gaze going down the corridor to the main entrance of the station house to where a soft, round little man in an expensively tailored gray suit entered vigorously. Bucher glanced at his watch; he had been in custody less than a quarter of an hour, and now silently wagered with himself that White Hat would have him sprung within the half hour. The round little man in gray could be his release.

The round little man in gray *was* his release—to the utter dismay of Homicide Captain Mack Whetson.

"Turn Bucher *loose?*" Captain Whetson boggled, incredulous. "Without charges? But Commissioner Evans . . . !"

"Now, now, Captain Whetson," Commissioner Evans soothed in a voice sugary enough to put a diabetic into shock. "I know what I'm doing." He turned to Bucher and thrust out a small pink hand with manicured nails. "Mr. Bucher, as Police Commissioner of this city I want to congratulate you most heartily, sir, on your conduct regarding those two vile creatures you confronted."

"But—but—!" Whetson burst out, half rising from his seat, his expression that of a man on the verge of unexpected and violent bowel activity. "Aside from killing two men, Bucher's gun is equipped with a *Gebracht* silencer, Commissioner; a *Gebracht* silencer is illegal even for *you* to own!"

"Tut, tut, Captain," Commissioner Evans clucked

confidently. "I'll take full responsibility for Mr. Bucher's actions here in the city, both now and in the future. You're free to go, Mr. Bucher. No charges. No charges whatsoever."

During the conversation between the commissioner and the captain, Bucher had been gathering his gear from the desk, and now he nodded his thanks to the pink, pudgy little man and strode from the room under the bewildered and angry stare of Captain Mack Whetson.

"Ah, Mr. Bucher," White Hat's stooped, weary-eyed director beamed happily in greeting some forty minutes later as Bucher entered the main compartment of the White Hat supersonic jet. "I trust Malloy and McGurk gave you no serious trouble."

Bucher shrugged indifferently, dismissing the subject as the big jet taxied around and, with a surge of power, shot down the runway.

"Your message referred to a matter of vital urgency," Bucher said, taking a seat facing the other man. The director nodded, his seamed face reflecting far more than its usual worry.

"Yes, Mr. Bucher. It is a matter of vital urgency."

"I'm not sure I understand the part of your message about a tranquilizing gas, though I may have decoded it improperly."

The director laughed thinly a tired sound. "I'm afraid that was my fault. I fear I failed to encode the message properly. The vital urgency I referred to concerns an antidote for a tranquilizing gas. Do you recall my mentioning the name Bruno von Kessler some time ago?"

Bucher searched his memory, but nothing clicked

15

into place. "Is that the Nazi armored division commander who gave the Allies fits during World War II?"

"No. But you're on the right track. They're of the same family—cousins, I believe—but much farther apart in political convictions. Bruno von Kessler was very much anti-Nazi, and not a military man. By profession a biochemist."

"Right." Bucher snapped his fingers, suddenly remembering. "This Bruno character fled Nazi Germany rather than work in one of Hitler's death factories."

The director nodded. "That is correct, Mr. Bucher. He fled Nazi Germany, went underground, and surfaced in Spain where he married a wealthy Spanish widow. When he was threatened with deportation back to Germany, he went underground again, along with his wife this time. They later surfaced in the United States where they were given sanctuary. Until recently Dr. von Kessler and his twenty-six year old daughter Isabella—the mother died in childbirth—have been living in St. Paul, Minnesota, where von Kessler is chief chemist for a national cosmetics firm.

"According to our information, Dr. von Kessler was obsessed with the idea of discovering, through chemistry, a means of ending warfare for all time—"

"So he comes up with this tranquilizing gas," Bucher said.

The director nodded. "He called it $H(g)A$-7 and sent a copy of his treatise on the subject to both the State and Defense departments. The Pentagon poohpoohed the paper, labeling it ridiculous. Their reason was that there is nothing new in the idea of tranquilizing gas as an invasion weapon in aggressive warfare, and I hazard the guess that every major power in the world has at least one, if not several. And, fortunately or otherwise, all of these have a number of things in common. Unlike phosgene, chloropicrin, mustard, and other irritant and corrosive gases, all tranquilizing gases in both liquid and gaseous form have common antidotes. Garlic, for instance. This lowly vegetable, which any gardener can raise in abundance with a minimum of effort, is the best antidote for all known tranquilizing gases. By chewing a few cloves of raw garlic any person can withstand the most effective tranquilizing gas. This in itself renders the use of tranquilizing gas absurd as an instrument of aggressive warfare."

"So what's the hitch?" Bucher asked. "How come the Pentagon pooh-poohed Dr. von Kessler's treatise on his H(g)A-7?"

"Because on the surface H(g)A-7 appeared to be just another tranquilizing gas. However, when the scientific data contained in von Kessler's treatise was analyzed, the Defense Department came to the shocking realization that von Kessler's formula was different from all other tranquilizing gases in one respect."

Bucher waited, saying nothing, a tiny chill of apprehension trickling up his spine.

"It has no antidote," the director at last said wearily. "Von Kessler did not disclose the antidote, nor even hint as to what the nature of such an antidote might be, and our people have failed consistently in their attempts to discover one. And believe me, Mr. Bucher, they have tried."

"Not even gas masks?"

"Gas masks are effective only against corrosives and irritants."

"But von Kessler knows an antidote?"

"It would seem so. At least in his treatise there is an indication that such an antidote exists."

"Then why the hell not ask him what it is?"

"Dr. Bruno von Kessler has disappeared, Mr. Bucher. So has his daughter, Isabella."

"And you want me to find him," Bucher said dryly, his tone touched with a hint of sarcasm. "And either get the antidote formula from him or burn the poor bastard."

"Mr. Bucher, H(g)A-7 comes in liquid form, but evaporates much faster than any known liquid, including human saliva, and its invisible, odorless vapor has the characteristic of combining with ozone, which is in all breathable air, and retaining its tranquilizing properties for several days. Moreover, our lab boys estimate that a mere gallon of the stuff is sufficient to tranquilize the entire city of New York."

"So? Perhaps the people of New York could do with a good tranquilizing—it'd give them a break from their madhouse rat race." Bucher waited for an answer to his question. At last he got it.

"Yes," the director said. "I want you to find Dr. von Kessler and get the antidote—and for heaven's sake don't let anything happen to the man until you do get it. If a gallon of H(g)A-7 can immobilize all the people of New York, a very few hundred gallons could immobilize the entire nation, and any aggressor possessing the antidote could march his troops across the country without meeting an ounce of resistance. Yes, and again yes. Find Dr. von Kessler and get that antidote at all costs."

"What's the Syndicate tie-in?" Bucher asked. "There must be one or you wouldn't have called me."

"Do you know a Syndicate character by the name of Nick Ferroni?"

"Hell, yes!" Bucher sat upright in his seat. "I've had a score to settle with Ferroni since . . . for a long time." To himself Bucher said: I intend to make the sonofabitch eat that golden earring he wears.

"Then the immediate problem is this, Mr. Bucher: find Ferroni. White Hat has received information that Ferroni got hold of the information concerning von Kessler's formula and, unlike our dear Pentagon, believed it at once."

"You believe Ferroni has von Kessler?"

"Yes."

"Where is Ferroni supposed to be now?"

"Unfortunately he has disappeared also, though we do know he boarded a plane for Paris yesterday." The director took a thick manila envelope from his coat pocket as Bucher asked somewhat in surprise:

"Are we on our way to Paris now?"

"Right." The director offered a rather limp smile. "And in this envelope you'll find all the necessary papers for entering France. One of our people is waiting at Orly Airport to contact you. A Ms. Yvette d'Aquitaine, I believe. Use Identification Code thirteen."

CHAPTER TWO

"M'sieur Bucher?"

Zephyrs of titillating perfume caressed Bucher's nostrils as he turned at the sound of his name being pronounced "Boo-*cheer*," and this fragrance, plus sight of the speaker, caused that familiar tightening in his loins. She was possibly thirty years old, though probably less, and tall for a woman, perhaps five-nine or ten, and willowy—long legs, a narrow waist, and full, ripe breasts that pressed against the material confining them. But her face impressed Bucher even more than her figure.

She stood at his elbow and looked directly up at him. Bucher caught his breath involuntarily: large green eyes, copper-gold hair burnished in rich waves, a sensible nose, and cherry red lips made for kissing. In the nick of time Bucher caught himself from going into a stagger.

"I'm Bucher," he managed.

When she spoke again, her voice was soft and throaty with a gentle, seductive quality that, for an instant, afflicted Bucher with a Neanderthal urge to crouch at the knees and howl with joy for being male.

"Aunt Agatha sends you her love," she said, "but told me your gift was superfluous."

Bucher nodded. Her inane words were the initial segment of White Hat's ID Code 13. He replied with the terminal segment grinning sourly; White Hat's ID codes were a bit of Hollywood B-grade he couldn't become accustomed to.

"Aunt Agatha's opinions have arthritis," he said.

"My name is Yvette d'Aquitaine," she smiled, her limpid green eyes casting as they stood there in the bustling terminal. "There is somewhere we can talk? But not here, non?"

"You name it," Bucher told her, gathering control of himself again. "Wherever you say."

"This man you seek, this Nick Ferroni, he is a habi-tué of La Monbrison Health Spa," she said, regarding Bucher dubiously, yet with something of a mischievous twinkle in the depths of her green eyes. "If you have no objection to going to this spa . . ."

"Good enough," Bucher said impatiently. "Where is it located?"

"Here. In Paris. Come, we will find a taxi."

They did not find a taxi, or even look for one. Bucher rented a blue Ford sedan from a pimply-faced young man named Hugues, according to his name plate, at the auto rental service in the terminal, and by following Yvette's directions reached Monbrison Health Spa in the north of Paris in less than an hour.

"There is another place this Ferroni frequents," Yvette said in her precise English as Bucher pulled into the spa's parking lot. "It is a bistro of ill repute down next to the River Seine. Its name in your language is the Bloody Cat, and it is also frequented by many Apaches."

"Right - on," Bucher replied. "If we don't find Ferroni at the spa, we'll try the Bloody Cat."

21

"Are you certain you have no qualms about visiting this health resort, M'sieur Bucher?"

"Why should I? Why do you ask?"

"Well," Yvette began hesitantly. "This resort has certain rules that—"

"That we will observe. I've got to find Ferroni and find him in a hurry."

"Naturally, M'sieur."

"What kind of a damn joint is this?" Bucher whispereded harshly to Yvette a few minutes later when the spa's hatchet-faced receptionist curtly ordered him to undress.

"Please, M'sieur," Yvette whispered in reply. "Do not let anyone hear you call Monbrison's a—damn joint. It is a most respectable and dignified establishment. The cream of Parisian society come here to relax."

"Relax? Naked? In public?" Bucher caught himself. "Yeah. Okay, okay." This was exactly the type of place that would have enormous appeal for Nick Ferroni, and he had to find Nick Ferroni in order to locate Dr. Bruno von Kessler. Still and all, Bucher reflected as he and Yvette undressed in the locker room, running around nude was a helluva way for him to do anything except show his ass.

"Mon Dieu, M'sieur!" Yvette gasped as Bucher hung up his garments. He turned toward her, P-38 concealed in a large towel, to find her staring at the scars from old bullet wounds on his body in a sort of horrified fascination. "Those scars, M'sieur. You have had many . . . adventures, non?"

"Come on," Bucher growled. "Let's get this over with. Going about naked is not my cup of tea."

Yvette could not make the same statement with any

22

degree of truth, Bucher thought to himself as they made their way into a huge compound in back of the building. She comported herself naked the same as if she were fully dressed. Even so, with a face and figure like hers, she'd be approached at least once, if not attacked outright, by every hardtail on the grounds.

"You Americans," Yvette teased fetchingly. "A great nation of Christians and yet you are miserably ashamed of God's greatest gift to creation."

"What gift?" Bucher cast a weather eye at a black-haired nymph prissing past; the word "Maverick" was tattooed in block letters from hip to hip below her navel.

"What gift?" Yvette said. "Why, the human body. What else?"

"Yeah," Bucher said curtly but feeling appropriately stupid. "That's right."

The play area—the entire compound—behind the building was at least five acres large, and all of it was surrounded by a thick stone wall twenty feet high. Beyond the vast swimming pool immediately at the rear of the building, a manicured lawn stretched to the back wall and sported a volleyball court, a tennis court, a miniature golf course, plus a number of other games that could be played by both men and women.

"To prevent creating a distraction and disturbing any games that might be in progress, sexual intercourse is not permitted on the grounds," Yvette told Bucher judiciously. "For that one must go inside; there are rooms upstairs."

"We're here to find Nick Ferroni!" Bucher growled defensively, already feeling as awkward and self-conscious as the wino caught masturbating in the Sanctum Sanctorum, and wishing to hell the receptionist had accepted the fifty dollar bill he had tried to bribe her with.

"Piff, M'sieur. I know why we are here." The mischievous twinkle in her green eyes was now more pronounced. "I am not inviting you to go upstairs with me."

"Right. Now you sashay around the grounds and see if you can flush Ferroni from the shrubbery while I stake out the back door if he tries to leave. I'll be there." Bucher pointed to a lawn chair off the west end of the swimming pool that would put his back near the high stone wall. "If you spot Ferroni, bait him past that chair."

"Bait him, M'sieur?" Yvette frowned. "How bait him?"

Bucher looked at her a moment in wonder before realizing she actually did not catch his meaning. He grinned crookedly. "Yvette, if what you're walking around with isn't enough bait to make any man jump off the Eiffel Tower, I'll join the Fraternal Order of Eunuchs."

She studied his face a long moment, then blushed prettily. "Sacré bleu, M'sieur Bucher," she murmured. "What a way you have of complimenting one."

Bucher watched the supple animal grace of her movments as she sauntered away, and knew from experience that he was looking at a superb athlete in the pink of condition. He groaned inwardly, though it was her feminine attributes, which had little to do with physical prowess, that caused him to do so.

Bucher stationed himself in the lawn chair, the towel-wrapped Walther in his lap, and ran sharp eyes over the Monbrison grounds. He counted thirty-five people present, excluding himself and Yvette, which meant that there was a "single" in the crowd some-where. A small group of people were entertaining themselves at the golf course, but most were gathered at the volleyball court where a lively game was in progress. To his right two elderly men labored seri-ously over a chessboard, while behind them two over-weight matrons sat knitting, contentedly engaged in small talk.

The compound enclosure had very little shrubbery, most of it a stand of rosa rugosa some thirty yards long and six feet tall running parallel to the swimming pool and equidistant between it and the compound's rear wall. Bucher watched Yvette pause a moment to kibitz the players at the volleyball game, then continue on until she reached the roses and passed from sight behind them. He wondered drearily how long he would be able to take the strain of Monbrison Health Spa and was humbly grateful for the towel.

Yvette had not yet reappeared from behind the rosa rugosa when the black-haired nymph with the word Maverick tattooed across the flat plane of her tummy prissed past again, giving Bucher a level stare. Bucher, not unaccustomed to having women stare at him, ignored the look, somewhat enraptured by the heady aura of nubility surrounding the young woman. He watched her until she disappeared inside the building, then hastily counted the remaining persons on the grounds. This time the figure was fourteen men and the same number of women, again exclusive of himself and Yvette, which probably meant that Maverick was the "single" he'd thought of earlier. Why? he won-dered. Why would a frisky young lass like Maverick be at a joint like Monbrison's without a male escort?

The small enigma was solved a couple of minutes

later when Maverick reappeared followed by two jokers who had gunsel written all over them. Both were fully clothed. Sonofabitch! Bucher cursed wearily to himself. He did not recognize either of the hoods, only the type. In his varied life he had seen too many two-bit triggermen not to know the stamp—and Maverick had been waiting at Monbrison's for only one reason. To finger Bucher the moment he arrived. And in case Nick Ferroni was not here at Monbrison's, as thus far the mutt obviously was not, then there would probably also be someone to finger him at the Bloody Cat.

Bucher did not puzzle over how Nick Ferroni knew he was in Paris, or that he would come to Monbrison Health Spa, for he knew without puzzling. Ferroni had had someone posted at Orly Airport waiting for him to arrive. For a man like Ferroni this was more or less basic, especially if he happened to be involved in some big wheeling-dealing operation.

"That's far enough," Bucher snarled in French when the trio led by Maverick were twenty yards away. Maverick squeaked in honest fright and scampered toward the volleyball game just as Yvette d'Aquitaine reappeared from behind the rosa rugosa. The two gunsels stopped and glowered malevolently at Bucher.

A chilly smile touched Bucher's hard face. The two bums exuded self-confidence, a trait he always liked to see in torpedoes he was about to get blood-gutsy with.

"Make your move, punks." The predatory snarl in Bucher's voice brought a start from the two elderly matrons, and the two old codgers looked up from their chessboard in surprise. From the corner of his eyes, Bucher saw swift movement in the direction of the rosa rugosa but dared not move his gaze from the

26

two hoods. One of them wore a gray suit, the other was nattily dressed in casuals and sported a flaming red necktie. Red Necktie would move first, Bucher decided, since he looked the more stupid.

In this Bucher was correct, yet the simple-minded jerk was so steeped in overconfidence that he moved so slowly it was laughable; at least to Bucher. Obviously neither of the punks suspected that a gun was concealed in the towel in Bucher's lap. As if reaching for a cigarette case in an inner coat pocket, Red Necktie leisurely raised his hand and reached under his left arm.

Since Bucher had just arrived in this country, he did not want to become embroiled with the French police, Yvette d'Aquitaine and White Hat notwithstanding, and therefore did not want to kill either of the hoods if it could be avoided. Thus Bucher waited until Red Necktie hauled his heater into view before making any move. Even then he only moved the towel in his lap a fraction.

"Koosh!"

It is doubtful if even the two elderly couples nearby heard the quiet sigh of the Walther, made even quieter by the towel. But they heard Red Necktie's bark of pain and surprise as his snub-nosed revolver flew from his hand and landed on the grass by the pool, yards away. They also saw him seize his injured hand with his free one and do a ludicrous, agonized jiggle, and heard the blistering Spanish curses pour from his lips.

Bucher already had Gray Suit fixed in a cold stare, but obviously the abrupt and unexpected course of events had put the man in a momentary quandary. The swift movement Bucher had noticed near the rosa rugosa moments ago now became Yvette d'Aquitaine.

27

He had not expected her, but her appearance did not really surprise him. She streaked over the grass on silent feet, speeding headlong for Gray Suit, who did not see her but seemed about to decide that he should not draw his iron after all. It was just as well. For him to have done so would have served him little purpose.

Red Necktie, still clutching his injured paw and cursing in Spanish, saw Yvette coming and fled as if all the devils in hell were on his tail. She cleared the ground in a powerful thrust of legs while she was still a good ten feet from Gray Suit. Bucher watched, thoroughly fascinated.

In the air Yvette doubled forward, knees drawn to her chin, feet to the fore, and, in passing in front of Gray Suit at shoulder level, kicked, again powerfully, the force of the blow greatly increased by the speed of her hurtling body. Her right foot struck a devastating blow on the side and front of his face.

Gray Suit staggered wildly, arms flailing in all directions like a windmill gone berserk, and his teeth came together with a loud clack. By the time he recovered his balance, Yvette was coming at him again, but this time on the ground. Gray Suit started violently in fear and surprise and prepared for flight but did not make it. Yvette came to a sudden stop three feet in front of the man and, both arms held rearward for balance, brought her right foot up from the grass to club the joker a bone-jarring blow on the side of the head.

Bucher simply shook his head in admiration. He should have known Yvette would be a master of Sabot, the deadly French technique of fighting with the feet.

Gray Suit pinwheeled across the grass from the blow, at last skidding to a halt on hands and knees and with a terrified whimper, jumped to his feet and raced for the exit after his departed comrade.

Bucher, assuming the hassle was over, was about to get to his feet when Yvette made a dash for Maverick. The tattooed woman shrieked in protest when Yvette locked the fingers of both hands in her black tresses, spun around, whipped Maverick over her shoulder, and slammed her down against the grass with a meaty, grunty thud. And then, as Bucher and all the others present watched in spellbound silence, Yvette kicked, slapped, biffed, and generally mauled Maverick, all the while speaking in low, indistinguishable tones Bucher assumed to be oaths, until the harassed young woman with black hair managed to break free and flee in frantic desperation.

Yvette stifled an impulsive giggle behind her hand as the other woman disappeared from sight, then strode nonchalantly toward Bucher, tucking a wisp of copper-gold hair behind one ear.

Bucher himself managed to maintain a certain degree of nonchalance, though with no little effort, as his eyes wandered from Yvette's face down to her ripe, upthrusting breasts that joggled maddeningly in rhythmic accompaniment to the movements of her body, then to the gossamer plane of her tummy and the immaculate thighs that could move hotly around a man's waist as . . . Bucher groaned inwardly a second time and literally forced his mind to other matters.

"Who were they?" he asked as the other nudists in the compound slowly commenced to move toward them out of curiosity.

"I do not know," Yvette said, an intrigued expression on her face. "I did not recognize either; you refer to the gunmen? They spoke Spanish but with a peculiar accent—"

"It was Mexican-Spanish," Bucher told her, also intrigued.

"Nor did I recognize the young woman who brought them into the compound. She could be a trollop from the Bloody Cat. The place has many trollops."

"Come on." Bucher rose to his feet and turned toward the building's rear entrance. "Let's get out of here before these people start asking questions."

While they were dressing, Bucher puzzled as to how the two thugs had managed to get past Monbrison's hatchet-faced receptionist with their clothes on when the woman had refused his bribe to permit him to do the same. Some minutes later, when he and Yvette were leaving the spa as police sirens drew nearer, he saw the answer to his puzzlement in the form of the receptionist's grossly swollen jaw and black eye. Even so, she looked at him in arch disdain in order to shore up her sagging aplomb and as if to say: "So what? I kept *you* from entering the spa with clothes on, didn't I?"

On the spur of the moment and despite the urgency of the situation Bucher leaned far across the desk in her direction.

"You didn't turn the other cheek," he accused her indignantly as Yvette squeaked with smothered mirth and clung to his arm. "Next time turn the other cheek."

The receptionist's mouth opened wide for a scream of alarm when Bucher and Yvette ducked out the door.

CHAPTER THREE

The Bloody Cat would never qualify as a tourist's idea of a Parisian cafe. In the first place it was not a cafe at all, but a bar whose culinary accommodations extended no further than a large barrel of pickled horsemeat from which huge sandwiches were made. In the second place it had no sidewalk appendage so dear to the tourist's and the Frenchman's heart. In truth, the Bloody Cat was an underground dive that came into being by way of refurbishment of an enormous cellar six feet below street level. It was a favorite of Parisian Apaches, the street faction of the city's criminal element.

"I must call Raoul and Pierre," Yvette told Bucher as they descended the steps. "Raoul and Pierre may know who the two gunmen are. And the young woman you call Maverick as well."

As they entered the place, the odor of stale tobacco smoke and sour wine smote Bucher's nostrils. It grew even stronger as he and Yvette advanced into the large room, some thirty feet wide and twice as long. The bar, almost as long as the room itself, stood near the opposite wall and faced the entrance. The large floor was bedecked with crude wooden tables and chairs, the tables covered with red and white checked cloths, and in the center of each an empty wine bottle supported a partially burned candle.

The Bloody Cat was completely empty except for one squat bartender, whose cagy eyes followed their every movement.

"Select a table," Yvette whispered to Bucher. "I will join you as soon as I telephone Raoul and Pierre."

Bucher almost stopped her, but did not. Why bother to stay when Nick Ferroni was so obviously absent?

He chose a table near the door, taking a seat that put his back to the wall, fanning the room with hard eyes as he did so. He did not like the Bloody Cat. Something was badly out of kilter here—as it had been since his arrival in France. Something stunk to high heaven, and not only with the Bloody Cat, but with the entire Bruno von Kessler caper. What in hell did Nick Ferroni want with von Kessler to begin with? What did the Syndicate want with an antidote for a tranquilizing gas? Perhaps von Kessler's daughter Isabella figured into the plot somewhere. Perhaps Ferroni, always the ladies' man, had gone overboard for daughter Isabella, though Ferroni had always prided himself on being seen only with beautiful women, and the photograph of Isabella von Kessler given to Bucher by White Hat's director had not predicted that von Kessler's daughter would develop into any striking beauty. Still, the photograph had been taken when the girl was ten years old, so one never could tell.

Bucher did not doubt that he and Yvette had been followed from Orly Airport to Monbrison Health Spa, and this meant that someone had been waiting at the terminal for him to get off the plane. Someone besides Yvette d'Aquitaine. But it simply didn't make sense for Nick Ferroni to have baggage clerks and other airline attendants on his payroll, as well as two Spanish-speaking gunsels on standby alert just in case Bucher happened to arrive in Paris. No one would have been waiting for him at Orly *unless they had known in advance* that he was due to arrive! Yet how could Ferroni have known he was even leaving the states when he himself had not know of it until White Hat's director had told him. And this had happened *after* the White Hat jet was already in the air.

A chill of apprehension washed over Bucher's big frame. If the Syndicate had managed to infiltrate White Hat, he was as good as dead. Then a wry grimace flickered over Bucher's hard face at the thought of White Hat being infiltrated, by the Syndicate or anyone else. No more than half a dozen people outside the organization knew of White Hat's existence, so infiltration was out of the question.

Nevertheless, something stunk! Something that he could no more put his finger on than he could fly like a bird, but it stunk.

And then, without warning, danger hackles stirred on the nape of Bucher's neck, and it came to him that the odor of tobacco smoke hung exceptionally heavy, even in the low-ceilinged room, for the room to be devoid of all persons save himself, the bartender, and Yvette, busy at hushed conversation in a phone booth at the far right rear of the room.

"Why did all your customers leave so quickly a few minutes ago?" Bucher demanded of the bartender, who replied with a stony stare, spat vindictively, then turned and disappeared through a door behind the bar. At that moment Bucher's attention was drawn in the direction of the telephone booth by the rapid tap-tap of Yvette's spike heels on the hard floor.

"Quickly!" she cried, knocking tables and chairs from her path as she raced toward the exit. "Up the stairs! Quickly!"

They raced up the stone steps three at a time, and when they reached the sidewalk, Yvette shoved Bucher toward the street corner twenty yards away. Bucher moved, growling when they reached the corner:

"What the hell's going on?"

There was no need for Yvette to answer. Bucher got his answer in an ear-splitting crack of thunder as splintered chairs and tables, red and white checked cloths, particles of broken glass, and a great cloud of foul dust and other debris gushed upward from the Bloody Cat's stairwell.

"That is what is going on, M'sieur," Yvette said in a tight voice. There was a strained look about her beautiful face, and it had lost much color. She spat an emphatic word in French. "He had the bomb waiting for us when we arrived."

Bucher guided her around the corner to where he had parked the rented Ford. "How did you learn of the bomb?" he demanded harshly. The possibility of Yvette d'Aquitaine being a traitor had crossed his mind, but he had discarded the notion as ridiculous. To his knowledge no White Hat operator had ever turned against the organization.

"Raoul," Yvette said promptly. "It was he I spoke with on the phone. Pierre was not there, but Pierre had told Raoul that the Bloody Cat was to be bombed this morning, and when Raoul learned I was calling from the Bloody Cat, he screamed for me to flee."

Bucher could not keep the sudden suspicion out of his tone: "Who is this Raoul and Pierre you keep mentioning?" Nor did he feel his suspicion unjustified. He had been in France less than two hours, and already two attempts had been made on his life.

They reached the Ford and got in before Yvette answered.

"In America I suppose you would call Raoul and Pierre gangsters," she began slowly. "Though they do not steal from others, and they do not shoot people. You see, in France today there are many commodities imported from Germany, Holland, Spain, and other countries, commodities that have grossly inflated and unrealistic prices simply because they are imported. Raoul and Pierre are importers, one might say. However, when they bring these commodities into the country, they do not transport them by normal channels and do not pay the high, unfair import tax the French government demands."

"You mean they're smugglers." Bucher eased the Ford out into the traffic.

"Yes, that is it! They smuggle." She laughed softly, the color returning to her face. "For a moment the word in English evaded me."

"Would you rather we spoke French?" Bucher was aware of feeling an immense relief—he had been suspicious of the lovely creature beside him without actually realizing it.

"I would not. I have not had such a beautiful opportunity to practice my English since leaving the convent."

"So what are Raoul and Pierre to you?"

"Well, among other things they are my informers. They have close ties with the underworld in Paris, and throughout France. They know everything that goes on in criminal circles, more or less, and they tell it to me. It is an excellent arrangement. They think I am employed by a private detective agency."

"Why do they tell you all these things?"

"Why? Oh, you Americans. I hope because they love me. That's why."

"Okay, okay," Bucher growled. He was not certain he understood what sort of arrangement Yvette d'Aquitaine had with her Raoul and Pierre, but since it appeared to be very personal, he did not want to pry.

For some minutes they rode without speaking. Then Yvette broke the silence.

"Are you not interested in the identities of the two men who tried to kill you at Monbrison Health Spa?"

"You *know?*" Bucher wheeled the rented sedan into the curb and slammed on the brakes.

"But of course I know. For what other reason would I have called Raoul and Pierre?"

"I'll be goddamned," Bucher announced blankly to the world at large, feeling somewhat like the man who hurried like hell to get there with something only to discover when he arrived that everyone already had plenty. "All right," he said at last, "who are they?"

"Carlos Rodríguez and Gustavo Sánchez."

"What?"

Yvette eyed him largely. "It is true, M'sieur. Raoul is certain. They were recently imported from Mexico by Jules Lurante."

"And who is Jules Lurante?"

"He is King—the Big Boss of the Paris underworld. He also owns the Bloody Cat."

"And where does this Lurante punk live?"

"He has a huge villa in St. Denis, fourteen kilometers outside of Paris. It is of great importance? I mean that the men were Rodríguez and Sánchez. Or that they were imported?"

"I only know them by reputation," Bucher said quietly, his thoughts racing a mile a minute. "They're two of the most bloodthirsty rats ever to come out of Mexico. Even worse than Simón Blanco, and he is accused of more than three hundred hits. Carlos Rodríguez and Gustavo Sánchez are two triggermen for el Roca, who controls the rackets for the Syndicate in northern Mexico."

"Dear God!" Yvette breathed. "What do we do now?"

Bucher made no immediate reply. Something was out of kilter again, something new. The two hitmen who had come to the health spa to chill him had not impressed him as being torpedoes of Rodríguez and Sánchez's reputation. Before he could answer, Yvette set him right.

"They are narcotic addicts," she said. "Raoul told me they are both mainliners."

"And Raoul had no idea why Jules Lurante imported them from Mexico?"

"You are well known to the French underworld and have a fierce reputation here in Paris. Perhaps Lurante had them imported to kill you because none of his own men would accept the task."

"Huh-uh." Bucher shook his head. "If any of Lurante's hitmen refuse the task, then they get hit themselves. That's the way the game is played. So Rodríguez and Sánchez weren't imported just to rub me out. No one outside White Hat knew I was coming to France. No one knew you and I were driving from the airport to Monbrison Health Spa, and then from there to the Bloody Cat."

Yvette studied his cragy face intently, thinking hard, then burst out: "Mon Dieu! What a foo-foo I am not to have remembered before now. Your name is on the rental papers for this car, and we were talking of the Monbrison Health Spa and the Bloody Cat and Nick Ferroni while the attendant filled in the information and found the key."

"That's *it!*" Bucher smote the steering wheel with a fist. He had wondered at the time why the pimply-faced rental agent—what was the bastard's name? Hugues?—had taken so long in the back office. "The crud was making a phone call instead of looking for a key."

Bucher looked back over his shoulder, waited for a large refrigerated truck to pass, then reentered the traffic behind it.

"We're going back to the airport?" Yvette asked quickly.

"You better goddamn well believe we're going back to the airport," Bucher snarled in icy fury. He rammed his accelerator foot to the floorboard, and the sedan leaped forward, careened around the refrigerated truck, barely missing one of the famous traffic-directing policemen Paris uses in lieu of traffic lights, and shot down the boulevard at top speed.

CHAPTER FOUR

The auto rental agency booth inside the airport terminal was not in the busy section of the building, but far down on one end away from the main flow of traffic. Hugues, the same attendant who had rented Bucher the Ford sedan, was still on duty. He was a young man of about twenty-five, with very buck teeth, a very bulbous nose, and a very severe case of acne. He donned his best customer-relations smile when he saw Bucher and Yvette approaching.

"Ahhh, Mr. Bucher. Through with the car already?"

"You jack-off son of a bitch!"

Crack!

Bucher's open-handed slap spun him completely around and flung him to the floor. Before he could recover and scramble to his feet, Bucher sprang over the counter on one hand. Hugues never made it to his feet. Bucher would not let him, but gathered a big handful of shirt and necktie up close to Hugues' throat and held him on his knees.

Bucher shook him and growled, "You know who I am, sonofabitch?"

Hugues blanched, neighed in terror, and broke wind in violent abandon.

Bucher shook him some more, and Hugues' teeth rattled like the sound of dice in a leather cup. "You know who I am, sonofabitch?"

"Yes, yes!" Hugues wailed. "They—they call you the B-Butcher!"

In a deft movement Bucher plucked out the switchblade that was sheathed to his left ankle. At the ominous sound of the seven and one-half inches of razor-sharp steel whipping into view only inches from his throat, Hugues' eyeballs bulged far out of their sockets.

"Right," Bucher snarled savagely. "I'm the Butcher—" he pressed the back edge of the blade against Hugues' juglar vein, "—and either you talk, and talk loud and fast, or else you get butchered. Which will it be?"

T-Talk!" Hugues squealed. "I'll talk!" He rolled his bulging eyeballs across the counter top toward Yvette in a desperate plea for mercy.

"Talk then!" Bucher rattled the man's teeth some more.

Hugues slithered an unwholesome-looking tongue from between fear-parched lips and slurped it around his mouth. "A man came by early this morning," he quavered. "He showed me a photo of you and gave me five hundred francs and told me to call him when you arrived at the airport. That's all."

"And you called him," Bucher snapped.

"I told him you had arrived."

"What else. Did he ask where I was headed?"

Hugues tried to nod, but Bucher's grip on his throat and his own position made it difficult. "I told him you and her . . ." again Hughes careened his eyeballs toward Yvette, "I told him I heard you and her talking about the Monbrison Health Spa and the Bloody Cat. And that's everything."

Bucher released his grip on the man's shirt and stepped back, but Hugues did not rise.

"Who was the guy?" Bucher demanded harshly. "Where is he now?"

"I don't know!" Hugues wailed, the slithering tongue wetting his parched lips again. "Him and the young lady—"

"What young lady?"

"I don't know." Then, blubbering and quaking, Hugues managed to describe Maverick to a tee.

"And did the man wear a small golden earring in his left ear?" Bucher asked.

Hugues nodded violently. "And when he gave me the five hundred francs and told me what I must do to earn it, he and the young lady left, but a few minutes later I saw the young lady talking to Simone, the ticket clerk in the third booth up the line."

Bucher stepped back and let Hugues get to his feet. Things were beginning to shape up. They were still fuzzy as hell around the edges, but they were beginning to shape up.

"Why, yes, M'sieur," the ticket clerk called Simone told Bucher some minutes later. "The young lady you describe purchased two tickets for San Luis Potosi in Mexico, according to the passenger manifest. One for herself and one for a Mr. Nick Ferroni."

"What was her name?" Yvette asked from beside Bucher.

Simone consulted the manifest again. "Smith. Mary Smith."

Bucher shook his head in mild dismay. San Luis Potosi was high in the mountains of central Mexico, and what'n hell would Ferroni be doing there? For that matter, what had the bum been doing in Paris?

Suddenly things were not shaping up as well as Bucher had thought. Suddenly he had a sort of scattered feeling—like the man with both hands full of loose ends.

Bucher purchased a plane ticket for himself, and then he and Yvette left the ticket booth. "Here's where you and I part company," Bucher said. "It was a short visit, but it sure as hell wasn't dull."

Yvette gave him a moody glance he was unable to interpret but said nothing until they were in the broad companionway leading from the terminal proper to the exit waiting room.

"I could accompany you," she said almost sullenly.

Bucher was about to suggest she do just that, but instinctively changed his mind. It would not work. With Yvette as his companion on this caper, on any caper, common sense told him he would be unable to apply himself fully to the task at hand; to any task at hand—except Yvette. That familiar feeling tingled in his loins. Christ! What a delightful, delicious task she would be. Perhaps they should have gone upstairs to one of the rooms at Monbrison's.

In the midst of this enthralling speculation, Bucher suddenly found Yvette in front of him; they collided gently, then she seized his biceps and shoved him not so gently into a tiny alcove between two giant support pillars of the companionway, out of the main flow of traffic.

"I said I could accompany you." Her jaw was firmly clenched, her entire expression depicted an aggressive determination Bucher had seldom seen in the opposite sex.

"I heard you the first time, Yvette," Bucher told her not unkindly. "But it wouldn't work. Instead of searching for Nick Ferroni, you can imagine as well as I how we'd spend the time."

She tried to shake him. "Do you find the idea of spending time with me in such a manner objectionable?" The anger she attempted to put in the question failed to mature.

"You know better than that." He took her in his arms, kissed the tip of her nose, and a faint giddiness touched him when she squirmed the long, golden warmth of her superb body against his.

"We should have gone upstairs at Monbrison's," she said miserably. "I wanted to."

"So did I," Bucher replied truthfully. "And if—"

"You *did?*" She brightened noticeably. "Honestly?"

"Honestly."

"But—but you acted so cold, so impersonal."

"It was only an act." Then he lied whitely. "I didn't carry the towel into the compound at Monbrison's only for the gun in it. You do things to a man."

She looked up into his eyes, studied his hard face for a long moment, then sighed heavily in resignation and said:

"Throughout the French underworld it is said that the Butcher never breaks his word. Is this true?"

"I try never to break it."

"Then promise to return to me in Paris as quickly as you find this Ferroni person." She attempted again to shake him, her arms about his waist. "Promise me! Otherwise I shall scream to the airport police that you are deserting me and our seven starving children. Such is a grave offense in France."

43

Bucher laughed in spite of himself. "Okay. I promise."

Her attitude changed immediately, her limpid green eyes sparkling with impish delight as she hugged him to her.

"Then I will wait for your return," she murmured demurely. "It will not be easy, but I will wait."

Bucher did not fly directly to San Luis Potosi nor even to Mexico, but stopped off at Houston, Texas, and rented a small, long-winged monoplane, which would be efficient at landing and taking off on short runways. His next stop was Matamoros, across the Rio Grande from Brownsville.

Years ago, when he was still crime overlord of the Syndicate's East Coast Division, Bucher had done a tremendous business in smuggled marijuana with his Mexican counterpart, Pepe Hidalgo, known throughout his domain as el Roca—the Rock. El Roca operated out of Matamoros and more or less under the aegis of the Syndicate, but Bucher's relationship with the man had always been as friendly as circumstances allowed, and el Roca was not the type who would let anyone else, and certainly not the Syndicate, dictate whom he could choose as friends.

Even so, Bucher reflected as he directed a Matamoros taxi to take him to la Cantina del Contento, to his knowledge the two goons who'd tried to gun him at Monbrison's in Paris—Carlos Rodríguez and Gustavo Sánchez—were on el Roca's payroll. Still, he could not see Pepe Hidalgo sending such punks after him, in Paris or elsewhere—unless Pepe wanted them bumped off.

The interior of la Cantina del Contento reminded

44

Bucher somewhat of the Bloody Cat; it had a low ceiling, was furnished with wooden tables and chairs, but without the wine bottles and candles, and the place was empty except for a man behind the bar, whom Bucher instantly recognized as one of Hidalgo's henchmen. The man recognized Bucher also, and a broad smile spread over his swarthy face.

"Ah, Mr. Bucher. It has been a long time since you visit the cantina."

"Hello, Juan. Where's the big boss?"

"Bucher!" A huge, mustachioed Mexican came quickly through the curtains covering a doorway leading in back and lumbered across the large room. *"Amigo!"* El Roca clasped Bucher in a rib-cracking bear hug that lifted Bucher off the floor, then released him and stepped back, his broad face an expression of comradely fondness. "And what brings you to the land of el Roca, eh?"

"Carlos Rodríguez and Gustavo Sánchez," Bucher said bluntly, eyes on el Roca's face for any telltale sign that he might be involved in any rub-out plans the Syndicate might have for Bucher. He saw none.

"Yucht!" El Roca's dark face formed in lines of strong disgust. "Carlos Rodríguez and Gustavo Sánchez? Those cabrones?" He took Bucher's arm. "Come. Let us sit at that table in the corner and have a drink. You still favor Gusano de Oro?" He waved to the bartender. "Juan."

"You look prosperous, Pepe," Bucher said as they sat down. He already knew instinctively that el Roca had nothing to do with the attempt on his life at Monbrison's.

Pepe Hidalgo gave the Latin's expressive shrug. "There are good times and there are bad. Now we are

45

having one of the good times here in Mexico—thanks to your Washington."

Bucher looked him a question as the bartender placed a bottle of mescal containing a large yellow cactus worm, a saucer of quartered limes, and a shaker of salt between them.

El Roca chuckled contentedly, continuing: "Your government gives my government millions of dollars to stamp out the cultivation of marijuana. Through a contact in Mexico City I have a contract to cut and burn fields of the stuff; they pay me by the hundred kilos destroyed, so most of my men grow marijuana and the rest 'discover' the fields and burn them. The operation is not very exciting, but it is very nice of your Washington. Also it is very lucrative. Of course, we do not burn all the marijuana. We ship a few thousand kilos across the border from time to time to prevent the scarcity from driving the price so high people will lose their taste for it, but we will not resume our big smuggling operations until the Washington money runs out." He poured two drinks of the fiery mescal and pushed the saucer of limes toward Bucher. "Now tell me, amigo," he said quietly. "What is this about the two men you spoke of? Carlos Rodríguez and Gustavo Sánchez."

"They no longer work for you?"

El Roca shook his massive head. "Not for over a year now. They went to the hard stuff: heroin, opium, and such. I hear they are now in the employ of Hernán Gris—a real bastard. One can no longer do business with Gris. He wants the cake and all the icing these days."

"Rodríguez and Sánchez tried to rub me out in Paris a couple of days ago."

"No!" El Roca looked aghast, incredulous. "Carlos Rodríguez and Gus Sánchez? Can you not be mistaken, amigo? Those two have no guts. If I owned burrows I would not let them be my stable boys since they went to the hard stuff. Perhaps they sold Hernán Gris a bill of goods, eh?"

"Perhaps Nick Ferroni did. He financed the try for me in Paris."

El Roca nodded solemnly. "So now the Butcher seeks Ferroni to wreak his terrible vengeance, eh?"

"I also have an old score to settle with Ferroni. That bauble he wears in his ear once belonged to a friend of mine. Ferroni killed her."

"Aye-yi-yi." The other grimaced in disgust. "I did not know Ferroni killed women also."

"Ferroni kills anything," Bucher growled. "It's the way he gets his jollies."

"So now you kill him."

"I must find him first. I'll appreciate any help you can offer in locating the bastard. He's in Mexico. That's all I know."

El Roca labored to his feet. "There is very little that takes place in Mexico that Pepe Hidalgo cannot learn of. Un momento, amigo. Let us see what a few phone calls will do."

"Start with San Luis Potosi. I also know Ferroni was headed in that direction."

El Roca turned rapidly for one of his bulk and looked sharply at Bucher. "The high country of the San Luis Potosi region is the land of Hernán Gris and his Nahuatl Indians, amigo. If Ferroni is tied in with Gris, you could encounter very much difficulty getting to him."

Bucher shrugged. "See what you can dig up."

While he waited for el Roca's return, Bucher sipped mescal and reviewed his progress thus far, which was practically nil. He knew only that Ferroni had left France for San Luis Potosi and damn little else. As yet there was no hint of Dr. Bruno von Kessler and his daughter Isabella. Even Yvette had made no mention of the doctor or his daughter, probably because she had been told nothing of them, told only that Nick Ferroni was to be located. Such was not an unusual procedure for White Hat. It made for tighter security.

Unaccountably, a series of scenes shoved themselves into the forefront of Bucher's thoughts as he sat there, mental images stemming from the possible consequences to a nation on which von Kessler's $H(g)A-7$ tranquilizing gas had been used. If the country should happen to be the United States, and if the gas were used by an aggressor nation who also had the antidote to von Kessler's $H(g)A-7$, according to White Hat's director such an aggressor could take over the country in a matter of hours.

Bucher killed his drink; the pictures coursing through his mind were anything but pleasant. Then he frowned in puzzlement. It was beyond his powers of comprehension why, for what reason, Nick Ferroni wanted von Kessler—assuming Ferroni had kidnapped von Kessler and had him stashed somewhere. Ferroni was nothing but a muscle man who had clubbed and clawed his way into the Syndicate hierarchy, and such things as tranquilizing gas and antidotes simply were not the Syndicate's bag.

Naturally it had occurred to Bucher that Ferroni might be after the same thing he was—von Kessler's antidote for $H(g)A-7$—except Ferroni would probably try to sell it to some foreign government for several million dollars. Yet in Bucher's opinion Nick Ferroni did not have the ability to pull off such a deal. Still, common sense dictated that Ferroni had not involved himself with von Kessler for the sport of it. Ferroni did not operate that way. Even so, a musclebound lout like Ferroni and a brain like von Kessler made strange bedfellows. Nevertheless, Ferroni—

"You were right, amigo," el Roca said, interrupting Bucher's thoughts as he returned and dropped heavily into his chair. "Ferroni has been seen numerous times around San Luis Potosi recently. He pretends to be vacationing, but my informant tells me this is not true, that Ferroni is onto something so big he cannot handle it himself and is possibly seeking the aid of Hernán Gris."

"Thanks." Bucher got to his feet.

"Wait! Wait!" El Roca threw up a restraining hand. "How do you travel?"

"A small plane."

The other shook his head vigorously. "Do you wish to announce to all the region of San Luis Potosi that you are arriving? A plane will never do. Planes are still rare in many parts of Mexico." He tossed Bucher a set of automobile keys. "In back of the cantina is my Land Rover, completely furnished and supplied— bed, food, water, everything. I keep it ready just in case I must make myself scarce in a hurry. Take it. It is ideal for a trip like yours. And of course I will not be needing it as long as the Washington money holds out. If I can assist you further let me know. My contact in San Luis Potosi is Señorita Leonor Delosa of the Hotel Anahuac."

Four hours later, on Mexican Highway 57 South, Bucher was less than twenty kilometers from San Luis Potosi when a hundred yards ahead he saw what he at first assumed to be a youth or a man of small stature staggering drunkenly along the edge of the macadam toward the speeding Land Rover. And, since Mexico has one of the highest per capita rates of alcoholism in the Western Hemisphere, Bucher detected nothing amiss until the vehicle was some twenty-five or thirty yards from the reeling, swaying figure. At this point, however, he noticed that the person was not male, but a young woman—about whom he sensed something decidedly familiar—wearing a man's oversized shirt and trousers, the fronts of which were covered with blood. Blood also covered her hands and virtually concealed her face. Yet the blood was not sufficient to hide the stark terror and pleading in her dark eyes.

Bucher slammed on the brakes, screeched to a halt, rolled from the cab in a thrice, and was around on the off-side of the vehicle by the time she reached it, sagged against it, clutching the open window for support.

"Help me!" she quavered in Spanish. "Please, before God, help me. They're going to kill me." A gusty, forlorn sob escaped her, and Bucher managed to catch her under the arms a split second before she hit the ground, unconscious.

Five minutes later he had her on one of the Land Rover's fold-out bunks, and as he washed the blood from her face and hands with water from the tank, the peculiar feeling that he knew the young woman, or that their paths had crossed somewhere in the past, continued to grow.

50

The wound responsible for all the blood was not nearly as serious as he had at first suspected—only a small cut high on the left temple. Any scar that it might leave would be hidden by her hair. She groaned when he washed the wound with antiseptic from the first-aid kit and closed it with gauze and a strip of adhesive. After swabbing the last traces of blood away from her face and hands, Bucher rose to his feet to look at her, trying to remember where he had seen her before.

She lay very quiet and still, her only movement the rise and fall of her plump breasts, exposed when Bucher had removed the man's cheap gray shirt to search for further wounds. He had found none; apparently the wound on the temple was her only one. She was barefoot and, as best he could tell, wore nothing but the baggy khaki trousers, which were no less than a dozen sizes too large and were held about her tiny waist by a short length of grass rope knotted in front.

Bucher shook his head, trying to jar his thoughts into line. His memory seemed about to tell him something concerning the young woman's identity, yet each time he tried to grasp the wisp of recollection, it evaded him. And of course there was the problem of what the hell he was going to do with the woman. He wanted to enter San Luis Potosí as inconspicuously as possible, yet any attempt to do so without attracting any attention would be defeated if he took with him a totally strange female who might well, on regaining consciousness, burst out screaming: "They're trying to kill me!" And if Bucher was any judge, she would soon be conscious.

Could he leave her here? Bucher shook his head.

He had no intention of dumping her back onto the road with someone trying to do her in. True, she was nothing to him—except that she was a fellow human being whose life was in danger. So leaving her where he'd found her was out, period. And yet . . .

Bucher climbed back into the driver's seat of the Land Rover and studied the map of Mexico he'd found above the sun visor. According to the map, he had passed the turnoff to a small, out-of-the-way village named Arista one or two kilometers back. He replaced the map and kicked life into the vehicle, then wheeled around to head back the way he had been traveling. Aside from San Luis Potosi, Arista was the closest town, and he could leave his unwanted passenger with authorities there for her own protection. Or at least until they learned who was trying to kill her, and why.

Bucher never made it to Arista. Half a kilometer beyond the turnoff and immediately after the Land Rover forded one of the small, crystal clear rivers often found in the central highlands of Mexico, noises from the rear of the vehicle reached his ears, and he stopped.

The young woman behind him was now seated on the bunk sobbing wildly and struggling with the handle of the rear door. When the Land Rover ceased to move, she whirled in Bucher's direction, teeth bared and ready to defend herself, unaware that the rope knotted about her waist to support her pants had come untied. As Bucher stared over his shoulder in perplexity, the larger garment slid silently down over her slender body to a crumpled heap around her ankles. Bucher stared, thunderstruck, for one split second, then quick as a panther was out of his seat and reaching for her. She tried to dodge, to evade him, but in the rather cramped quarters of the Land Rover's living section there was nowhere to go.

Without ceremony Bucher seized her arms, flung her back onto the bunk, and seated himself on the edge of it to prevent her from getting up.

But she didn't try to get up. All she did was curl into a tight, naked ball, sobbing hysterically. Bucher let her cry. In truth he had no choice. In her over-wrought emotional condition any attempt to calm her would have been wasted effort. A full quarter hour passed before her sobs subsided, and suddenly she squirmed around to face Bucher on an elbow.

"Go ahead, you m-murderer!" she gritted in flawless English. "K-Kill me and get it over w-with!"

CHAPTER FIVE

"Go to hell," Bucher growled to hide his surprise. "Or maybe you'd best go to the booby hatch; you act like a nut. Are you?"

She relaxed slightly and stared at him sullenly. "What are you doing here?"

Bucher shrugged and decided to play it her way to offset the possibility of her pitching another hissy. "You imply that I'm here to kill you."

"W-Well, aren't you?"

Bucher shook his head. Whatever else she might be, she was also a spunky wench. "I don't kill women."

"But you kill. I know your reputation."

"I only kill when I must, to stay alive." He made an impatient gesture. "Let's not get involved in personal philosophies." He was about to ask her a question that had bugged him all the way from Paris, but she interrupted hotly.

"Where are we?"

"Somewhere between the main highway to San Luis Potosi and a small village called Arista and—" he looked out a side window, "—more precisely, we're parked in a huge stand of large mesquite trees beside a small river."

"Why?" she insisted, still hotly. "Why are we here?"

"We were on our way to Arista, where I hoped to find protection for you while I went about my business—until I recognized who you are and pulled in here."

Her eyes held his fixedly. "You know who I am?" she whispered.

"Not your name, but I know you tried to finger me for the rub-out at Monbrison's in Paris a couple of days ago. When you dropped your trousers, this told me." He pointed to the word 'Maverick' stretching across her naked belly from hip to hip.

Bucher saw it in her eyes; only then did she realize that she wore nothing except the khaki pants tangled about her ankles. Again she curled into a tight ball, attempting to conceal her nudity with forearms and hands.

"Oh!" she gasped desperately. "Oh!"

"Easy, easy," Bucher said not unkindly. "Rape never was my thing."

She succeeded in squirming back into the trousers without leaving the bunk, faked him a dazzling smile, and in a very unladylike manner sweetly cooed: "Horseshit!" Then, gritting: "From my brief but despairing experience, you professional killers are all alike. First you want to—to—molest any female you can get your hands on, then you want to kill."

Bucher ignored the unfair remark. "Why did you finger me at Monbrison's for Carlos Rodríguez and Gustavo Sánchez?"

She gave him a startled look. "You knew who they were?"

"I do now. What I don't know is why."

"I was forced to do it. Honest."

Bucher believed her. "By Nick Ferroni?"

"You know—" she gulped, "—that vile beast also?"

"We molest-minded killers all belong to the same union."

"Ferroni told me you'd been sent to find my father and kill him," she said contritely. "And that if I didn't do exactly as he said he'd tell you where my father was. That's why I fingered you."

A short, sharp charge of excitement shot through Bucher. Heretofore he had simply assumed the young woman on the bunk to be a gun moll belonging to Ferroni & Company, but the remark about her father suddenly put an entirely different light on the matter. He took her face in both hands, studying it intently and remembering the ten-year-old girl in the photograph he had been given by White Hat's director. She had the same pert nose, generous mouth, the same fine, intelligent dark eyes . . . It was an unbelievable, a truly fantastic stroke of luck.

"You're Isabella von Kessler," he said barely above a whisper.

She frowned, pulling free. "I thought you knew me!"

Bucher sat back shaking his head. "Only as Maverick, not as Isabella von Kessler."

"Why do you want to kill my father?"

"For one of your intelligence, that's a stupid question."

"What's intelligence got to do with it?" she flared. "I'm scared silly. For me and for my poor father."

"Dammit, I don't want to kill your father! I don't want any harm to come to him, understand? Or to you, for that matter." He took a deep breath and mentally crossed his fingers, hoping for the best. "Where is your father?"

Suspicion sprang to life stronger than ever in her dark eyes. "Why?"

"H(g)A-7."

Isabella's eyes grew large with surprise. "W-Who are you?" she asked quietly. "Some sort of undercover agent? Nick Ferroni and the others call you the Butcher, a professional killer."

"My name is Bucher," Bucher said almost wearily. "And as I've said, I never kill except to stay alive. That's a man's obligation to himself—except where Nick Ferroni is concerned. I could kill him without remorse."

Isabella straightened with interest, clearly beginning to believe she had found a powerful ally, and swung her feet over the edge of the bunk to sit beside Bucher. "You're going to kill Nick Ferroni?"

"Maybe. You haven't answered my question. Where's your father?"

"I don't know where my father is. Somewhere in Mexico I suppose, otherwise why would they have brought me back here? And there has been a lot of talk about San Luis Potosí." She sighed heavily, a shudder shook her small frame. "These past few weeks have been nothing but one nightmare after the other."

"Who beat you up?" Bucher asked.

"Carlos Rodríguez and Gustavo Sánchez. They held me and tried to molest me." Blood-red anger creeping up her neck and over her face turned her olive complexion a deep crimson. "And they almost succeeded. But they took some kind of narcotic and forgot about me for a few minutes. I found these old clothes and fled."

"Where did all this take place?"

"I don't know—about half a mile from where you

57

found me, I think. There's a small cluster of adobe huts, five or six, off the main highway about a hundred yards."

Bucher was on his feet headed for the front of the vehicle by the time Isabella finished speaking. She watched him a moment, then asked:

"Where are you going?"

"To those adobe huts for Ferroni."

"Ferroni isn't there. Only Rodríguez and Sánchez and a handful of natives. Ferroni left us in Mexico City when we returned from Paris."

"Maybe Rodríguez and Sánchez know where Ferroni is. Your father also."

"They don't know *anything*. Except molesting and narcotics and killing."

Bucher spoke over his shoulder. "Who else is at the cluster of 'dobe huts?" He did not want to barge in on a dozen of Ferroni's killers.

"No one except four or five natives. Indians, I think."

Bucher nodded to himself. It figured. The Indians just might be some of Hernán Gris' Aztecan Nahuatls el Roca had spoken of. The possibility that Ferroni had tied in with Gris was becoming more obvious.

Isabella climbed forward into the seat beside Bucher as he switched life into the Land Rover.

"Now listen carefully and do exactly as I say," he told her as they emerged from the mesquite trees and reforded the river, headed for the main highway. "You stay inside the cab when we get to those adobe huts. And if the action gets hot, get down on the floorboards and stay there, understand?"

Isabella looked at him solemnly, large-eyed. "By action do you mean shooting and killing?"

"Right."

She forced her eyes straight ahead and swallowed hard. "I understand. But what I don't understand is why all of a sudden am I trusting you?"

Bucher gave her a wry grin. "It's simple. You've got no choice."

"But you could turn out to be another Rodríguez or a Sánchez. Or worse than both, though that's hard to imagine."

"Perhaps you do have a choice after all," Bucher said, strangely enjoying himself. "So who'll it be. Me or them?"

Isabella gave him a wary look, but also a half-smile. "Huh-uh. It's like you said at first; I've got no choice." She still wore nothing but the large trousers, having neglected to cover the upper part of her body on coming forward from the rear of the Land Rover, and now, as the vehicle moved over the rough, unpaved road, Bucher discovered the jiggling of her plump breasts proved to be an enticing distraction. He brought the Land Rover to a halt just before reaching the main road.

"Look," Bucher said in response to her questioning glance. "I can understand why you wouldn't want to put that bloody shirt back on, but get in the rear and dig around for something to cover those up." He pointed to her breasts.

She gave him a haughty stare. "A woman's breasts are for the suckling of the young. They are *not* to be construed as sex objects."

"Did you learn that from Rodríguez and Sánchez?"

"Oh, mercy!" She quickly scrambled out of sight.

"Look in one of those built-in drawers above the bunk. The guy who lent me this truck probably has some extra clothes there." Bucher spoke without turning, and a minute later Isabella crawled back up front beside him again.

"Will this do?" she grinned. "Does it quell your animal lusts?"

Bucher laughed in spite of himself. Under her arms and extending all the way to her waist, she had tied a huge red bandana.

"I don't know who lent you this Land Rover," she said seriously when he finished laughing. "But whoever he happens to be, he has a small arsenal above the bunk."

"There!" Isabella said some minutes later, pointing to half a dozen small, rundown adobe structures to the right of the main highway. "That's them. Turn right there."

The buildings were those small blocklike affairs one comes across in the most unexpected places in Mexico and frequently sees in the ancient Pancho Villa movies. Altogether there were six, one the inevitable cantina. Bucher braked the Land Rover to a halt fifty yards from the first building and had no more than done so when two vaguely familiar figures, now in T-shirts and trousers and each with a gun in his hand, emerged from the cantina to stop on the porch.

"It's them." Strong fear was very noticeable in Isabella von Kessler's hushed whisper. "Carlos Rodríguez and Gustavo Sánchez."

"Which is which?" Bucher asked.

She looked at him oddly, the fear also in her eyes. "I thought you knew them."

"I do, by sight and by name, but I still don't know

60

which is which—not that it makes a damn bit of difference now."

"The one on the left, the shorter of the two, that's Rodríguez."

Bucher pushed open the door on his side. "Stay here. And if things get too hot, hit the deck and stay down."

Isabella's only reply was a nod. Some of the color had left her face, yet there was a defiant cast to her features as she stared in loathing at the two men on the porch of the cantina.

Bucher stepped out of the vehicle and away from it, knowing from experience that the fireworks would soon start and wanting to draw it away from the young woman in the truck.

"The Butcher!"

It was Rodríguez who spoke. The words carried clearly from the sagging porch and brought with them a certain quality of exultant gloating. "This time there'll be no slip up."

Never once removing his bleak eyes from the pair, Bucher moved slowly toward the cantina. He stopped twenty-five feet from it.

"I got no hassle with you boys," Bucher said evenly in fluent Spanish. "All I want is Nick Ferroni and to know where Dr. Bruno von Kessler is. Where are they?"

Rodríguez goosed Sánchez in the ribs with an elbow, sniggering gleefully. "All he wants is to know where Nick and the doctor are."

Sánchez did not share his cohort's high spirits, but stood glowering threateningly at Bucher. "I am about to repay you for what happened in Paris, scum," he snarled.

61

Bucher made no immediate reply. At a time like this there was little that could be said, though he was aware of the real reason behind Sánchez's venomous attitude. It was Gustavo Sánchez whom he had classified as Red Necktie at Monbrison's Health Spa, thus it was Sánchez that Yvette d'Aquitaine had roundly clobbered, and the fact that the man had been bested thoroughly, and before witnesses, by a member of the opposite sex had, to Sánchez, placed a question mark on his cherished *macho* and knocked his bloated masculine Latin ego for a loop. And because he considered Bucher to be the cause of it all, he now glowered at Bucher menacingly in virulent hatred.

Bucher shrugged mentally, admitting to himself he had expected no less from the pair, and it would be Sánchez who made the first bid. Nevertheless, it was their choice, not his. Even so, a barely perceptible weariness stole over him, and faintly the bitter-sour taste of defeat came to his tongue.

"You want to know where Nick and the doctor are, Señor el Butcher?" Carlos Rodríguez said in mock politeness. "Very well, I will tell you. They are somewhere in Mexico." Paradoxically, this struck Rodríguez as comical, as if he had coined some gem of incredible wit. "And you may search for Nick and the doctor without fear for your life, Señor el Butcher gringo cabrone. In Paris, Number One instructed Nick that you are not to be killed; only captured. This because Number One desires the enormous pleasure of killing Señor el Butcher gringo dog in person."

Instantly, instinctively Bucher became more alert. Number One? Who was Number One? Why would this Number One want to kill him personally? White Hat's director had said nothing about anyone as-

62

sociated with the Bruno von Kessler case being called Number One.

"Number One wants no part of me." Bucher spoke confidently, as if he knew the identity of the person. "The bum has no more guts than a yellow cur."

Surprisingly, Rodríguez and Sánchez looked at him in dismay for a moment, then burst into hooting laughter. Bucher waited, watching, never once taking his eyes off the killer duo, but wondering at their laughter.

Then Gustavo Sánchez made his bid. With practiced ease the semiautomatic in his hand whipped up to line on Bucher, and the man—

"Koosh!"

—slewed drunkenly sidewise, brains exploding out the back of his head as the silencered Walther that had appeared in Bucher's hand loosed its hushed death sigh. The sledgehammer force of the hundred thirty-eight grain, nine milimeter slug streaking through Sánchez's skull flung him so far off balance that he wheeled clumsily in a half circle and pitched off the porch to the sun-baked earth in front of the cantina, dead before he hit the ground.

Carlos Rodríguez was no less determined than his partner. His gun arm snapped forward toward Bucher and—

"Koosh! Koosh!"

Rodríguez staggered as though kicked by a burro. The two P-38 slugs struck an inch apart on the left side of his chest, lifting him up and back, his shoulders striking the batwing doors of the cantina. He landed in a limp, lifeless heap, legs sticking out onto the porch under the batwing doors. One leg jerked violently, once, but from a muscular spasm, for he too was dead before he hit.

63

Bucher chanced a glance toward the Land Rover as he leathered his piece, and saw the stark white face of Isabella von Kessler, dark eyes huge, starring at him in a sort of rapt, fascinated horror.

Cautiously, Bucher made his way to the cantina. The sound of a rear door reached his ears when he mounted the porch. He stopped, casing the area, and saw across the top of one of the huts two men and four women in peon garb fleeing frantically into the chaparral beyond the buildings. Still cautiously, Bucher pushed through the batwing doors and entered the cantina. The caution was unnecessary. The place was deserted.

During the next quarter hour he searched all the buildings and found them deserted as well. Yet in the hut that had obviously been used by Rodríguez and Sánchez as sleeping quarters, he discovered something out of the ordinary. This was in the form of a complete outfit for making home movies, including a battery-powered projector, a small screen, and even a can of developed film. To find such equipment in a place like this was in itself unusual enough, but knowing it had been in the possession of the two dead gunmen made it truly exceptional. Bucher's curiosity leaped to the fore. He loaded the entire outfit into the Land Rover.

"W-Where are we going now?" Isabella asked in a strained, little-girl voice as Bucher climbed in behind the wheel.

Bucher hesitated in starting the engine. His destination was still San Luis Potosi, but the course of recent events gave him pause. The two men and four women who had fled the cluster of huts knew he had killed Rodríguez and Sánchez—though whether they would notify the authorities was a question—and the Land Rover certainly could be identified, so it would be far better if he did not proceed directly to San Luis Potosi in daylight, but wait for dark and enter the city by another route.

"We're going back to that big stand of mesquite trees beside the river and hide until nightfall," he said, starting the motor. "Then we'll go on in to San Luis Potosi. Perhaps I can find a plane to take you back to the states."

He wanted to be rid of the young woman beside him. Without being told, he knew full well that once he reached San Luis Potosi and went on the prowl for Nick Ferroni, the going would get rough as last year's cob, and he could not afford to have Isabella von Kessler hampering his movements.

After they had again forded the small river, Bucher drove so deep in among the mesquite trees, camoflaging the vehicle so completely, it was doubtful that it could be seen even from the air. All during the trip from the huts Isabella had said nothing, but the color had returned to her face, and the fascinated horror in her eyes when she looked at Bucher had been replaced by something far more complimentary.

"I'm not going back to the states without my father," she announced quietly as Bucher cut the motor.

He regarded her levelly for half a dozen heartbeats before replying, then said: "Suit yourself, but we separate in San Luis Potosi. I've got a job to do and—"

"And you're afraid I'll be in the way. Is that it?"

"That's it exactly. Myself I take care of, but looking after you could cause complications."

Isabella caught a quick breath. "If you were in my place would you fly back to the States and safety knowing you were leaving your father in the hands of cold-blooded killers?"

It was a good point, Bucher admitted to himself, and well made.

"Isabella—"

"I can handle a gun, either rifle or pistol. My father abhors violence, but he claimed the world is so unsettled every person should know how to defend himself properly. And there are several pistols and rifles in back. Also several hand grenades. Let me stay with you. I won't be a burden, honest. I promise."

Bucher had no defense against the pleading tremor in her voice. "Okay, goddammit," he growled. "But the going might get hairier than hell."

"Do you think it's been a picnic for me thus far?" Intentionally she gave him an enigmatic little grin. "Besides, you haven't told me what you want with my father's H(g)A-7."

"There are a number of things you haven't told me," Bucher parried. "Like why you bought plane tickets only for Ferroni and yourself for San Luis Potosi in Paris. Who bought Rodríguez's and Sánchez's?"

"They already had theirs. They were about to return to Mexico when you arrived in France."

Remembering what Yvette d'Aquitaine had told him about Rodríguez and Sánchez being imported by Parisian underworld kingpin Jules Lurante, Bucher said: "I heard they were called to Paris to do a special job."

"Huh-uh." Isabella shook her pretty head. "Not from what I overheard them say. They went to Paris to act as bodyguards for Nick Ferroni; we all four flew over together. Ferroni was summoned to Paris by some person they kept referring to as Number One, who sent a small suitcase of U.S. currency to Ferroni at the hotel in Paris. I suppose that's why Ferroni wanted bodyguards." She funny-faced Bucher with a delightful grimace. "There's also a big supply of food-stuffs in back, and I'm starved. Can't we eat while we talk?"

CHAPTER SIX

They ate standing near the rear door of the Land Rover, the meal consisting of canned V-8 juice and canned corned beef made into sandwiches on canned whole wheat bread. The juice was unchilled yet nonetheless highly palatable to both of them for, like Isabella, Bucher was also hungry, having eaten his last meal the evening before in Houston, Texas. They were well into their second sandwich when Bucher asked:

"How did a crumb bum like Nick Ferroni get wind of your father's tranquilizing gas?"

Isabella, fetchingly ludicrous in the huge red bandana and oversized trousers, swallowed her food before replying.

"Father made no attempt to keep his discovery of the gas a secret; he was quite proud of it, in fact. That's the reason he published his discovery in *Science of Tomorrow* when the Pentagon rejected it. I suppose Ferroni learned of it that way. Through the science journal. In any case, one evening early last month Ferroni came to our house in St. Paul, told us he had been sent from Washington, that the Pentagon had changed its mind, and that father was to accompany him that very evening; he had a plane waiting at the airport.

"Father was overjoyed, and frankly, so was I. When

I insisted on coming along, Ferroni made no objection, and, well, when we stepped off the plane we were in San Luis Potosi. Father was furious when we learned of the deception. Then they separated us. That's all I know."

"But Ferroni took you to Paris with him," Bucher said.

"I know. And that still puzzles me. Why he took me I have no idea. At first I figured he had ideas of . . . molesting me, but I was mistaken. He never made a pass, never tried to touch me." She made a sound of loathing. "Thank God."

On this last Bucher offered no comment. He saw no good to be served by telling Isabella that Ferroni had probably taken her to Paris for the purpose of using her in the hideous manner which, in Syndicate jargon, gave him his jollies.

"And you don't know why the mysterious Number One gave Ferroni a suitcase full of money?" he asked.

Isabella shook her head. "I only overheard him say on the phone to someone that he had received the money from Number One. Nothing more."

"Does the name 'Hernán Gris' ring a bell?"

"Heavens, yes!" Isabella said almost wearily. "He's all Rodríguez and Sánchez could talk about half the time; Don Hernán this and Don Hernán that. He has something to do with the underworld here in Mexico. San Luis Potosi, I think." She sighed, laying aside the remains of her sandwich. "Poor Father. He worked so long and so hard to develop $H(g)A-7$, dreaming to stop war for all time, and his discovery so far has brought nothing but trouble." She entered the Land Rover through the rear, speaking over her shoulder as she did so. "There's nothing but men's clothing here, and it's all too big. Do you suppose we can get to San Luis Potosi before the stores close so I can find something respectable to wear?"

"Perhaps," Bucher told her, then hoping against hope that she could answer the question, asked: "What's the antidote for your father's H(g)A-7?"

"Only father knows. That's something he wouldn't tell even me."

Bucher frowned in disappointment, though her answer was not entirely unexpected. Dr. von Kessler had probably intended to keep the antidote secret to use the knowledge as an instrument of bargaining power, though any such intention would be useless with Ferroni. Nick Ferroni had ways of making the stubbornest man reveal his innermost secrets.

While Isabella was rummaging about inside the vehicle hoping to find more suitable clothing, Bucher decided, as a security measure, to case the area covered by the mesquite trees. The task took twenty minutes. He had not expected to find any threat to their safety, nor did he. The dirt road leading from Highway 57 turned at a sharp angle immediately after crossing the river, and he found no buildings in sight as he toured the perimeter of the trees which grew lush and green down to the water's edge. Nor was the water as shallow above the ford as he had assumed it might be, but formed a pool several yards across and about six feet deep. Moreover, the mesquite trees began again on the far bank of the river, as thick as they were on the bank where he stood. All in all, he could not have asked for a better place of concealment to lie and wait for nightfall. Satisfied, he picked his way through the trees back to the Land Rover, coming to an abrupt halt of surprise when he reached it.

Isabella von Kessler was the cause of this surprise. The red bandana and the oversized trousers were gone; she had found other clothing in the Land Rover, though not what Bucher would have expected. Instead of the former ridiculous attire, she now wore a white sarong hastily constructed from a sheet off the bunk—which, on her, looked anything but ridiculous.

Being only human, and virile male at that, Bucher simply stared. The only word applicable to Isabella that came to his mind right then was "exquisite." She was that, and devastatingly so. Odd that he had failed to notice before that even on tiptoes the crown of her midnight tresses would barely reach his chin, or that her waist was so tiny he could easily encircle it with both hands and have room to spare. She was so perfectly formed, Bucher was smitten with the brief conviction he was gazing upon some master sculptor's finest work of art.

"Gol-*ly*," she said with a shaky little laugh and blushed profusely in pleasure. "I'm glad rape isn't your thing."

The words jerked Bucher back to himself. "Sorry," he said brusquely, advancing the last few steps to the vehicle. "I didn't mean to stare."

Since she had witnessed Bucher's fearless confrontation and subsequent victory over Rodríguez and Sánchez, Isabella's personal opinion of him had undergone a remarkable change. Instead of a foe, she now considered him a fellow comrade-in-arms, whom a kind Fate had called forth to join her in doing battle against a common enemy. Therefore, in replying to his statement that he did not mean to stare, Isabella's tone took on a mischievous, teasing quality.

"You weren't staring, Bucher," she chided. "You

were boggling, mouth agape and all agog, eyes popping and tongue wagging." Behind a quick hand, she giggled impulsively and a bit self-consciously. "And since we're laying it on the line, I loved it, so there. For what it's worth, you may look at me like that any time you please."

Bucher gave her a wry grin. "Aren't you afraid I'll suddenly turn into a Rodríguez or a Sánchez and molest you?"

"No," she said honestly, soberly. "I'm not. It's funny, really, but . . ." She paused, frowning, and chewing gently on her lower lip.

"But what?"

"I . . . trust you. And don't ask me why. It's just there. Most women can usually sense it; I'll bet you never have forced yourself on a woman." The mischievous, teasing quality returned to her voice, sparkling also now in her dark eyes. "But it might be interesting."

"Maybe. But this seems hardly the time or place to discuss it." Bucher went around to the driver's side of the Land Rover and took a folded map from above the sun visor.

"You may be right." She followed along behind him. "For that matter—" She interrupted herself. "I'm beginning to suspect being right is characteristic with you. But I have something of a fatalist's outlook, probably due to my half-Spanish, half-German ancestry, and I'm inclined to think whatever is to be will be. My father is in grave danger—I'm sure of this—and I'm going to do everything in my power to help him so we can return to our home in St. Paul, but while I'm waiting for things to get underway, like us going on to San Luis Potosi, I don't believe I should spend my time weeping and wailing in sackcloth and ashes, do you?"

When Bucher failed to respond to this, Isabella continued, seeming to take heart from his silence. "Have you ever read that Russian historian's—I think his name was Tsenyetskov—have you ever read his account of the Russians' battle of Kiev against the Nazis in World War II?"

Bucher glanced at her with a negative shake of his head. "What's your point?"

"My point is this: The poor besieged Russians were worn to a frazzle; freezing, starving, barely hanging on and their strength slowly being sapped by the battle —later not one admitted to harboring any hope of living—yet on the eve of an upcoming attack that not one Russian expected to survive, they had time for each other."

A puzzled crease formed on Bucher's brow. "Had time for each other? I still don't get it."

"Oooooh!" Isabella stamped a small, bare foot in irritation. "They had time not only to talk about it, but to *do* it!"

"You mean to make love?" Bucher felt foolish even as he asked the question.

"Oh no!" Isabella said with enormous disdain. "Not to make love. To play chess. Didn't you know all Russians are addicted to chess?"

"Okay," Bucher growled defensively. "You made your point; the Russians made love in the heat of battle."

He unfolded the map, spread it out on the seat, and spent the next half hour familiarizing himself with the terrain surrounding the plateau city of San Luis Potosi. The city itself was at an altitude of more than sixty-five hundred feet, with mountain peaks jutting upward into the sky on all sides. El Roca had mentioned Hernán Gris and his Nahuatl Indians; Isabella had said Rodríguez and Sánchez had referred to Gris many times, and if Nick Ferroni was in cahoots with Gris also, locating Dr. Bruno von Kessler and getting to the man could prove a dangerous problem, especially if they were ensconced in the mountains surrounding the city. El Roca had also said Señorita Lenora Delosa, at the Hotel Anahuac in San Luis Potosi, was on his pay-roll as an informant. Thus the Hotel Anahuac, Bucher decided, would be his main stop.

During the time Bucher was busying himself with the map, Isabella had entered the rear of the vehicle and was now apparently asleep on the fold-out bunk. Bucher folded the map, replaced it above the sun visor, and quietly, quickly, slipped away through the trees. It had been in his mind since first seeing the pool above the ford, and, after making a second hurried scout of the area even though he was positive there was no danger of discovery, he went directly to the bank of the pool and shed his garments.

Thanks to the altitude and despite the intense heat, the water was deliciously cool and refreshing, and Bucher made his way to the deepest part, where the water reached to the base of his neck, and felt the tensions and tiredness begin to flow from his scarred body. It was habit with him to sleep very little while flying, therefore on the journey to Paris he had passed most of the time looking moodily through a window near his seat. He had been enjoying the water for the better part of an hour when a small sound from behind him caused him to turn quickly.

"Louse," Isabella grinned accusingly. "You could

have invited me to come along." Because of her shorter stature, she was treading water only a yard away. "You didn't have to sneak away."

"I thought you were asleep," Bucher told her. Her improvised white sarong lay beside his garments on the bank.

"You just assumed," she said, treading closer. "You didn't bother to make certain. Will you tell me something?"

"Like what?" Bucher asked warily.

"Like do I have some sort of invisible leprosy that only you can see?"

"This isn't Kiev." Bucher was not aware of any particular effort on his part to avoid her, though now as he considered the matter, he could easily understand why she might have thought so. "And we're not Russians."

Isabella gave him a thoroughly baffled look. In the total of her twenty-five years she had had only one affair, and that a brief but torrid one with a young professor during her final year in college. At the end of the term her young professor had packed his bags and without so much as a by-your-leave departed for parts unknown, never to be seen or heard of by her again. With Isabella the affair had not been one of casual dalliance, and when she at last recovered completely from the biting shame of the professor's ungenerous conduct, she discovered that she derived a sort of perverse joy from flaunting her feminine charms to male admirers until they became excited to the point of desperation; then she would coldly brush aside their fervid pleas with taunting laughter. Therefore the baffled look she gave Bucher now was not so much inspired by him as it was a reflection of the dismay she felt at herself.

"You know something," she said quietly in self-wonder, not looking at him as she spoke. "It could be that I'm a trollop at heart and am just now realizing it." Then her dark eyes found his and held them. "And you know something else? You're right. I followed you out here to the pool hoping to—to . . ." A deep crimson spread over her lovely face. "But at least I'm honest and open about it; I'm telling the truth. It was on my mind when you left to come out here, but I couldn't decide whether to join you, so I sat there through that entire reel of film, watching those horrible—" Her face went blank, for a second became a feminine caricature of suspended animation.

"Oh, my God!" she suddenly gasped. "I'd forgotten completely. That home movie outfit and film you took from Rodríguez and Sánchez's quarters back at that little village. Apparently the film is of an experiment with Father's tranquilizing gas used on some natives here in Mexico."

Bucher lunged for the bank. "Let's go."

"Bucher!" Isabella seized his arm.

"Yes?" He could not hide the impatience in the word.

"Please don't hate me, Bucher," she continued with a limp smile of apology. "I know I'm not a trollop unawares, but . . . but . . ."

Under the water Bucher circled her tiny wast with an arm and briefly drew her to him—and for damn certain he was not unaware of the gossamer caress of her vibrant, scented flesh against his. "Let's go look at the film," he grinned. "And then . . ."

CHAPTER SEVEN

In its entirety the film was seventeen minutes long
and contained two distinctly different scenes, both
with the same setting; a low-ceiling adobe room
furnished with nothing except five crude wooden
chairs. In the first scene an adult Mexican in peon
garb was bound securely to each chair. Of these five
occupants, three were women: an ancient, toothless
hag, a matron in her mid-thirties, and a young woman
who looked to have attained the full bloom of woman-
hood only recently. Of the two male occupants, the
older was a hulking broad-shouldered, meaty-faced
brute with small, beady eyes, the other a much younger
man, and handsome except for an ugly scar on his left
cheek.

These five were the only characters of both scenes,
except for some sixth person who remained off camera
save for a hand that, at the beginning of each scene,
held a calendar marked May in front of the camera,
and immediately thereafter, in the first scene, placed
a stone bowl filled with a colorless liquid on the floor
in the center of the circle formed by the five occupied
chairs. The first time the calendar appeared, the fifth
of May had been heavily circled with a grease pencil;
the second time the thirteenth of May was similarly

77

circled, indicating the particular date on which each scene was shot.

To set up the projector and small screen to view the film, Isabella had unfolded the other bunk in the Land Rover, thus forming a sleeping platform completely across the vehicle, with her and Bucher seated on the edge next to the rear door. After they watched the film twice, Bucher sat with his elbows on his knees and his head down, an open bottle of tequila Isabella had dug from the food supply in one hand, cold, clammy sweat dotting his furrowed brow. Isabella hunkered facing him, face pale, eyes huge.

"Wh-What do you think it means, Bucher?" she at last whispered fearfully.

"What did your father test his tranquilizing gas on?" Bucher's voice sounded strained and strangely foreign, even to his own ears.

"Guinea pigs."

"Not on humans?"

Isabella shook her head. "Only on guinea pigs. What does it all mean?"

"If that stone bowl of liquid contained $H(g)A$-7, and I'm strongly inclined to believe it did, it means your father discovered a chemical compound that effects guinea pigs as a tranquilizing gas, but its terminal effect on human beings is another kettle of fish altogether—you saw what took place in that second scene."

"Yes," Isabella said, still whispering. "I saw." Without warning a hard tremor shook her small body, and she leaped free of the vehicle to the ground outside.

Bucher made no move to follow and console her, but remained seated on the bunk, swigging from the bottle of tequila as the sounds of her violent dry-retching grated on his ears. Even so, when she reappeared and resumed her former place some minutes later, her color, along with her composure, had returned.

"I'm sorry you got saddled with a nutsy like me, Bucher," she said at last.

"Forget it," Bucher growled in sympathy. "That second scene would unnerve most people."

In the second scene of the film the occupants of the adobe room had not been tied to their chairs, but were free to move about as they pleased, and the heavy wooden chairs were now broken to pieces, as was the stone bowl, and scattered over the floor. The five occupants stood at various points about the room, simply stood there motionless as if frozen in place, all staring directly into the camera.

On seeing this Bucher had immediately sensed something grossly amiss, yet he had not actually recognized what it was until he stopped the projector and studied the scene as a still shot. And when recognition came, with it came a hot, sweaty nausea that lurched greasily in his stomach, for in each of the five pairs of eyes staring into the camera he saw unmistakable, stark madness.

At this point Isabella had buried her face in her hands, but when Bucher began rolling the film again, she had raised her head in time to see the hulking, older Mexican man pick up the heavy leg from one of the chairs and calmly, indifferently, beat the old hag's brains out. Nor did the old woman lift one finger in defense. The big man followed her when she collapsed and never stopped his powerful blows until her head was a bloody mass of crushed bone and shredded flesh. The horror was repeated three times more, with each of the three remaining occupants in the small room, and when he had finished with the last, the big man commenced brutally beating himself across the skull with the heavy chair leg, while his meaty countenance warped into a hideous mask of soundless, insane laughter.

Again Bucher pulled at the bottle of tequila, then corked it, and placed it carefully on the floor, his thoughts in seething turmoil. The information garnered from the film, presumed and factual, had thrown him for a loss. After his brief hassle with the automobile rental agent Hugues in Paris, he had felt as if things in the von Kessler caper were shaping up. Minutes later, on talking to the airline ticket agent Simone, he had felt like a man with both hands full of loose ends, and now, after seeing the film, he had a very decided impression of being completely lost.

If von Kessler's $H(g)A-7$ induced madness in human beings, as he felt certain it had, the destructive potential of the gas staggered the imagination. And if he didn't wind up the case in short order, that destructive potential could well cease to be a potential and become a reality on a mass scale. Thus it was essential that he get his ducks in a row, as it were. That he sort out and evaluate these new aspects of the case by straightening out his thoughts—at the moment the thing he needed most was to think—think—think! Toward this end Bucher crawled onto the double bunk and stretched out full length, face down, head in his arms.

"Bucher—" Isabella began.

"Be quiet!" Even though this sharp command had the ring of impatience, the words also revealed a fatigue Bucher did not acknowledge. Yet the long and relatively sleepless flight from Paris, plus the delicious relaxation from the time spent in the pool, plus the

tequila, now compounded to produce a result he had not foreseen. In less than two minutes after telling Isabella to be quiet, he was sound asleep, snoring softly.

In the pool, when Isabella first mentioned the film, they had rushed back to the Land Rover in such great haste and anxiety, both had neglected to dress, and now, deep in slumber, Bucher never knew it when Isabella wriggled her small, naked body in close against his and joined him in dreamland.

Dusk was descending over the land of the Feathered Serpent when Bucher awoke quickly, silently, at once in command of all his faculties and wondrously refreshed. He lay on his back, arms outflung, and Isabella, who had awakened some minutes previously, lay with her head on his shoulder. When Bucher gathered himself to sit up, he found a small, determined palm pressed against his chest; the determined look in her dark eyes in no need of interpretation.

"But we've got to get to San Luis Potosi," he insisted half-heartedly.

"We'll get to San Luis Potosi." She nipped his chest playfully with feverish lips. "But first I get molested."

They stopped for half an hour at a sidewalk clothing stall on the outskirts of San Luis Potosi. When they continued on their way, Isabella wore a pair of jeans, a sleeveless slipover blouse, a pair of sandals, and a light cloth jacket, the jacket to conceal the snub-nosed .38 revolver and shoulder rig Bucher had taken from the small arsenal el Roca carried in the Land Rover.

"Where are we going first?" Isabella asked, scooting across the seat to sit as close as possible beside Bucher.

Night had settled in solidly, even before they had left the mesquites beside the river, but the night lights along the busier streets of the city were sufficient to reveal the breathless wonder of her face and the worshipful glow in her dark eyes each time she looked at Bucher. When he failed to respond to her question, she repeated it. "Where are we going first?"

"First to the telegraph office," Bucher said, for the moment deserting his deeply troubled thoughts. "Then to the Hotel Anahuac."

Their stop at the telegraph office was wasted effort; it was closed for the night, and Bucher swore in silent disappointment on discovering this. His purpose in seeking out the office was to wire White Hat of his suspicions that von Kessler's $H(g)A-7$ only appeared on the surface to be a tranquilizing gas, while in truth it was a chemical compound that caused insanity in human beings.

Lady Luck was more generous at the Hotel Anahuac, however. El Roca's San Luis Potosi agent was not only at the hotel but owned it, and when Bucher and Isabella entered, was on duty at the desk.

Señorita Leonor Delosa was a hefty, large-breasted woman of forty with pronounced Indian features. Her small, piercing, coal-black eyes studied Bucher implacably in silence for some seconds after he introduced himself. Then she smiled, which completely transformed her stolid features.

"Pepe phoned me from Matamoros to say you might contact me," she said through her smile. "What can I do for you, Señor Bucher?"

"You are familiar with underworld activities here in San Luis Potosi?"

Señorita Delosa nodded slowly. "More familiar than

82

most who are not of the underworld. Pepe pays well to be kept up to date on everything of interest here. Hernán Gris is boss of this region, and Pepe hates the man with a passion. Gris is a hideous savage, and according to my informants, is now becoming involved in some new enterprise with one of your American gangsters, a Nick Ferroni, whom Pepe also mentioned is a man you seek."

"What is Gris' new enterprise?" Bucher asked tersely.

"That is a great secret, Señor Bucher, but Gris has been overheard to boast—the man is a compulsive braggart—that he has a project underway that will, in Gris' own words: 'avenge all peoples on the gringos of the North,' meaning your United States, of course."

An icy chill spread through Bucher. With Hernán Gris full of hate-America venom and in possession of the knowledge of how H(g)A-7 was produced . . .

To Bucher's mind the antidote to Bruno von Kessler's so-called tranquilizing gas was no longer of any great importance. The problem now was to find von Kessler, learn how much H(g)A-7 had been manufactured, and destroy it, the means of producing it, and anyone who got in his way. He took the photograph of Dr. Bruno von Kessler given him by White Hat's director and handed it across the desk to Señorita Delosa.

"Have there been any reports of an elderly man of this description seen in the company of either Gris or Ferroni?" Beside him Isabella grew tense with anxiety.

Señorita Delosa studied the photo in thoughtful silence, then asked: "He is an American?"

"Yes," Isabella said quickly. "It is my father."

"I have not inquired after such a man," the older woman said. "But I will do so. Is it important?"

"Very important," Bucher told her.

"Where will I find you?"

"Here," Isabella put in, glancing at Bucher for confirmation. "We'll take a room here at the Anahuac."

Bucher slid half a dozen large bills toward Señorita Leonor Delosa—many times the cost of a room, the surplus for the big woman's assistance. "Now," Bucher asked. "Where can I find Nick Ferroni and Hernán Gris?"

"Ferroni I do not know, unless he is with Gris, and Hernán Gris has a rancho near the village of Ajo, in the isolated Nahuatl Indian regions up in the mountains east of San Luis Potosi." Señorita Delosa paused, looking from Bucher to Isabella, then back. "Señor Bucher, if you go into this region and are captured by the Nahuatls, we will never see you again. I do not know to what end you seek this Ferroni and Gris, but if you are taken by the Nahuatls I am certain we will never see you again."

Bucher chewed this over in his thoughts a moment, then asked: "What's with the Nahuatls?"

"They are Aztecan, a sect of religious fanatics who cling doggedly to the legend that their Messiah, a blond-haired god with fair skin, will return and avenge all the wrongs, real and imaginary, done the Nahuatls, by anyone, over the centuries. The legend is more or less a common one, the world over, but the Nahuatls are very fanatic, and they are in Hernán Gris' employ."

"How can Gris get along with the Nahuatls?"

"He is part Nahuatl himself, and with money. Gris is very rich and the Nahuatls are very poor."

84

"If Gris is boss of the criminal element here," Bucher said slowly, "but lives in Ajo, he can't maintain his control in San Luis Potosi without some flunky to represent him locally. Who is that flunky?"

Admiration reflected in Señorita Delosa's small black eyes. "Don Pepe told me you are a man of great macho." She nodded her approval. "You hope to force Hernán Gris to come to you, am I not correct?"

"If possible," Bucher said grimly. "Who's the flunky?"

"Pablo Rojas. He owns the Diablo, San Luis Potosi's biggest nightclub. It is on Calle Juárez."

"Do you know the identity of Number One?" Bucher asked.

"No. But my informants hear often of this Number One. And more frequently as time passes, yet they hear this Number One spoken of as a foreigner."

"American?"

Señorita Delosa shrugged, gathering the bills from the desk. "Number One's nationality is not known, only that he is not of Mexico."

"You stay here," Bucher said to Isabella, who had been standing tensely beside him. "I'll return after I talk with this Pablo Rojas character at the Diablo."

"No!" Isabella almost shouted the word in her nervousness.

"I'll be back within an hour," Bucher insisted. "It could be dangerous at the Diablo."

"No!" Isabella gritted. "I will not be left behind. Where you go, I go. If you face danger, I will share it. I will not be left behind."

Bucher frowned his disapproval, but forsook the subject to avoid an argument—she would remain in the Land Rover when they reached the Diablo, even if he had to tie her hand and foot.

Bucher's thoughts were too engrossed with the task ahead to notice how readily, and meekly, Isabella agreed to wait for his return in the Land Rover when they reached the Diablo, otherwise he would have been suspicious. As it was, he noticed nothing unusual when he left the vehicle parked across the street near a small jardin and strode toward the nightclub. His plan was simplicity itself. He intended to beat the hell out of Pablo Rojas, wreck as much of the Diablo as possible, and thus draw Hernán Gris into San Luis Potosi. Thanks to Isabella, the plan worked without a hitch.

The Diablo differed from the usual Mexican cantina in that it employed a large number of pretty playgirls as an additional inducement to ensure the patronage of its clientele. One of these girls accosted Bucher the moment he entered the place.

"Ahhh, Señor Americano," she cooed professionally, eyeing the expensive cut of his garments. "You are alone, no?"

"Where's Pablo Rojas?" Bucher growled in Spanish.

Something went out of the young woman's face, and she became wary at the mention of Rojas' name. Even so, the fifty dollar bill Bucher gave her vanished into the cleavage of her low-cut blouse, and she pointed toward a flashily dressed man in his late thirties. He was seated at a table separated from the rest of the Diablo's main room by a divider.

"There," the girl said in scarcely audible words. "That is Pablo Rojas."

Bucher fanned the large room with his eyes. There were very few customers; less than half a dozen men engaged in quiet conversation with their favorite playgirl of the moment, and not one of them had the stamp of "bodyguard," which Bucher had expected to find. He nodded in silent satisfaction; so far so good. Now to clobber one Pablo Rojas and leave behind a message for Hernán Gris.

Bucher threaded the fingers of his left hand through the brass knucks in his coat pocket as he rounded the low room divider and made his way toward Rojas' table. A questioning glint appeared in Rojas' cold eyes at Bucher's approach.

Pablo Rojas had clawed his way up the success ladder of the Latin American underworld by the aid of cold-blooded animal cunning and a total disregard for human life. Thus he was a man enormously feared in criminal circles, and rightly so. Before Simón Blanco had been apprehended, Blanco had been Rojas' pet executioner, a fact that had given birth to a gallows-humor localism that stated that no man was Pablo Rojas' enemy for long; Blanco murdered them.

On reaching Rojas' table, Bucher leaned across it, simultaneously lashing out with his mailed left fist. The vicious blow flung Rojas to his back on a neighboring table. Bucher was on the man like a duck on a june bug, slugging, chopping, hacking, the blows devastating yet with only sufficient power to rend flesh and draw much blood. Bucher did not want to cripple the man. Rojas would serve no useful purpose if he was totally incapable of functioning, and Bucher had a message he wanted Rojas to deliver to Hernán Gris.

An awesome hush had settled over the Diablo, the hush interrupted only by sounds of the furious but one-sided hassle—mostly painful grunts and sobs of surprise and angry protest from Rojas, whose face quickly began to resemble a sculpture in hamburger.

Bucher desisted with the brutal mauling only when he saw the man was on the verge of losing consciousness. Rojas lay on the floor in a bloody, crumpled heap, sobbing wildly, unashamedly, amidst a torrent of silent vows to destroy, to utterly crush from the face of the earth the big, granite-faced cabrone who had attacked and utterly humiliated him. He, Pablo Rojas, would discover the identity of the bastard in the gringo-cut clothes and . . .

Pablo Rojas was to exert no effort to discover Bucher's identity. It was unnecessary. Bucher told him who he was. He seized the beaten man by the nape of the neck, lifted him bodily off the floor and snarled:

"When Hernán Gris asks who clobbered your ass, tell him it was the Butcher. Tell him me and my boys are taking over his operation here in this part of Mexico, and there's not a damn thing he can do to prevent it." With this he flung Rojas back to the floor and—

"Crack!"

—he whirled toward the bar to see the lone bartender drop a huge horse pistol and grab his shoulder. Isabella stood in the doorway of the Diablo, snub-nosed .38 in her hand. Her soft laughter sounded oddly out of place as she wrinkled her pert nose at Bucher.

"I told you I could use a gun. The bartender had ideas of shooting you in the back."

The bartender fled out a rear door, wounded shoulder streaming blood, as Bucher rounded the end of the bar. Bucher let the man go. His purpose was not to argue with hirelings, but to create such a commotion with Hernán Gris' lieutenant and the Diablo that Gris would come boiling into San Luis Potosi with blood in his eyes.

Toward further promoting this end, and with a large bungstarter from under the counter, Bucher strode up and down the bar, methodically smashing all the bottled goods on hand. When this was completed to his satisfaction, he opened all the beer barrel spigots and, as a final gesture, smashed the huge mirror that ran from one end of the bar to the other.

Not a syllable of protest was uttered by any of the customers or their playgirls as Bucher was wreaking this havoc, nor did anyone speak when he threw the bungstarter at Rojas and walked casually to the door. On reaching it he turned, addressing those in the room.

"When Rojas recovers, tell him I'll be back in a day or two to give him more of the same." With this he turned Isabella toward the door, and they left the Diablo, less than ten minutes after Bucher had entered it.

"Gad, *hombre!*" Isabella squealed in delight and admiration as they drove back to the Hotel Anahuac. "You're a one-man wave of destruction." Suddenly she sobered. "But why did you do it? And why did you tell Rojas who you were?"

"To bring Hernán Gris to San Luis Potosi. Rojas is nothing but a muscle man with not much smart, else he wouldn't be Gris' hey-boy. When Gris gets word of what happened he'll come hustling into town, thinking I'm here to start a gang war and take over his territory. Defending his territory is something he can't trust Rojas to do, because Rojas might defend it in such a way that would make him top dog and leave Gris out in the cold wondering what happened. That's the way the game is played. Now it's Gris' move, and I don't think he'll be long in making it."

CHAPTER EIGHT

Señorita Leonor Delosa was still behind the desk when they returned to the Anahuac, and Isabella, in glowing Spanish, gave her a graphic description of the incident at the Diablo. The big woman's broad brow was furrowed in deep thought when Isabella finished.

"Then I will have my informants posted to watch the Diablo for Gris' arrival," she said to Bucher, taking a key from a drawer of the desk. "This key is for a small house I own on the outskirts of the city." She hastily drew Bucher a crude but sufficient map, writing down the address. "It is best you stay there tonight instead of here. It is the house Don Pepe uses when he comes for a visit. Your vehicle can be hidden in back of it; there are many lime trees and a tall hedge. Return here in the morning. I should have learned something by then. Gris is not one to dally when his empire is threatened."

"How does Gris stand with the local police?" Bucher asked.

"He owns enough high officials to function without interference."

"And you?"

Señorita Delosa's face broke into a huge grin. "And I also. It is a survival technique Don Pepe taught me."

90

Bucher nodded in understanding. He would not be surprised to learn that el Roca owned at least a few of the very police officials Gris thought he had in his pocket.

"Here." Bucher dug a hand under his shirt and pulled a flat pack of hundred dollar bills from the money belt about his waist, then gave them to the older woman. "That's five thousand in extra grease for the cops. Lard it on anyone you deem necessary. There is one thing I must know in the morning— where can I find Señorita von Kessler's father. This is vital. A must. Take this picture." He gave the woman across the desk the photograph of Dr. Bruno von Kessler. "Show it to your contacts, and tell them there is a thousand dollar bonus for the one who can direct me to this man in the morning."

"Aye-yi-yi, Señor Bucher. So much money. Don Pepe told me you are a man who gets things done in a hurry. I am beginning to understand how." She looked at Isabella. "This photo of your father; it is a recent one?"

Isabella nodded. "It's only a few months old. It's an exact likeness."

"Good." Señorita Delosa shook her head briefly in wonder. "With five thousand American dollars I should be able to perform miracles before sunrise. But go now, and quickly. And use back streets. Pablo Rojas will be insane with hate and lust for revenge. Go now before he gets his men on the streets."

They went—but not to the house for which Señorita Delosa had given Bucher the key.

"But why not?" Isabella wanted to know as they pulled away from the Anahuac.

A dozen blocks or more went by before Bucher

answered. "Because I got work to do," he said harshly, then, in softer tones, continued: "It's work that won't wait. Not the way I see it."

"What sort of work? What's to be done before Señorita Delosa hears from her contacts?"

Again several blocks went past before Bucher replied. "If I've got Rojas figured right, he's already sent my message to Gris," he said at last. "And if I've got Gris figured right, he won't waste a second in coming to San Luis Potosi."

"And then what?" Isabella demanded in wide-eyed indignation. In her mind she had outlined other plans for them at Señorita Delosa's little house that night.

"Gris will know where your father is," Bucher snapped impatiently. "And finding your father happens to be first on the agenda right now."

"Oh . . ." She sighed wearily in self-chastisement. "I guess I'm something of a self-centered bitch at times. If—" She stopped short as Bucher wheeled into a poorly lit side street and slammed on the brakes.

"Isabella!"

"W-What?"

It had just occurred to Bucher that Dr. Bruno von Kessler might also be the mysterious Number One. "Did your father ever give any indication of being at odds with his adopted country?"

"With the United States? He did *not!* Why? Are you suggesting he might be behind all this?"

"Is it possible?"

"No. Not with Father, Bucher. It simply isn't possible. If you knew Father you'd understand. Non-violence is a religion with him; a serious religion. Why did you stop so suddenly?"

"We're there. The Diablo is just around the corner and down the street. Here's what we'll do . . ."

Isabella protested heatedly when she learned that her part of Bucher's plan required her to remain behind in the Land Rover.

"Keep the damn motor running!" Bucher insisted, and only then did she relent. "We might have to cut out of here in one helluva rush."

"You'll hurry back?" she pleaded.

"That depends on Hernán Gris. I've got some questions the sonofabitch might not want to answer. Wait here."

Bucher did not go directly to the Diablo, but cased the place from the small jardin near where he had parked the Land Rover on his previous visit. From this distance the Diablo seemed strangely deserted. The lights were still on, since it was still relatively early in the evening, yet he was unable to detect anyone inside, neither customers nor playgirls nor anyone else. That no police were present was testimony in itself of the degree of influence Rojas, and Gris, had with the local authorities, yet the hell he had raised in the joint less than an hour ago should have attracted the attention of *someone*.

Very cautiously Bucher moved around the jardin, alert for the unexpected, a characteristic trait with him always, but especially so when he was uncertain of the lay of the land or somewhat confused by circumstances of the moment. And for one of the few times in his life, Bucher was becoming more confused with each passing hour. This von Kessler case was developing a maze of perplexing aspects for which he could find no cause and no explanation. Not only did he view himself as a man with both hands full of loose ends, but was beginning to see himself as a man who was running after his shadow in an endless circle. Something concrete and viable *had* to pop before long, else he might start howling at the moon in utter dismay.

The single-story Diablo was sandwiched between two other buildings, the one on the right a story higher. And it was the second story of this building that presented Bucher with a solution to the enigma of entering the Diablo unnoticed, for this building sported the evidence of combined Spanish-Mayan architectural influence—an outside stairway leading to the room.

A quarter of an hour later Bucher lowered himself to the roof of the Diablo and moved on silent feet across the flat roof to the set of stairs leading down into the bowels of the building. Halfway down the steps he stopped, listening intently. He heard nothing other than the normal, expected sounds of the night and, after waiting a couple of minutes longer, he shucked the P-38 from under his arm and continued downward toward a dim glow of light at the foot of the steps. When he reached bottom, he found himself in a storeroom with two doors, one opening onto the main part of the Diablo and the other, whence came the light, opening onto the Diablo's small office. Still moving silently, Bucher advanced toward this partially open office doorway.

Pablo Rojas sat slumped backward in the chair behind a cluttered desk, his battered face bloody and discolored, yet it was not the condition of the man's face that shook Bucher, for he was responsible for its condition, but Rojas' overall condition. Rojas was as dead as yesterday's newspaper, and he had died in a manner Bucher had not seen since his years in the Syndicate.

Rojas' blood-streaked and bulging eyeballs protruded so far from their sockets that they appeared to hang outside his face, at the top of his cheeks, and the bloated, purplish tongue thrust forth from fiendishly grimacing lips. These were the grisly proof that the garrote buried in the swollen flesh of his neck had done its work well. Rojas' wrists, bloody and raw, were tied fast to the chair he sat in. So were his feet. Bucher stood motionless, viewing the scene, frowning in thought.

Death had descended so quickly that Rojas had not had time to wash the blood of Bucher's beating from his face and hands. Therefore, Bucher reasoned, Rojas' executioners had been waiting for the man when he returned to the office immediately following the beating. Bucher touched the dead man's arm; rigor mortis had not yet set in. Very likely, Bucher told himself, Pablo Rojas had been dead by the time he and Isabella had returned to the Hotel Anahuac.

Bucher gave the small office a quick, thorough search but found nothing he considered of value related to the von Kessler case or H(g)A-7, or even to Hernán Gris for that matter. Not a little puzzled by the death of Gris' chief henchman, he left the Diablo by the same route he had taken to enter it. He had been roundly mistaken in assuming Gris would come charging into San Luis Potosi to protect his interests. Bucher now doubted that Gris would come at all, for the very simple reason that Pablo Rojas had been too busy dying to dispatch a messenger to Ajo.

"It seems like I'm forever asking the same questions," Isabella said when Bucher related his findings to her some minutes later in the Land Rover, "but what does it all mean?"

"It beats me," Bucher told her honestly. "It beats me like the very hell." Since joining White Hat he had encountered some doozies, but this case was developing into the granddaddy of all enigmas.

And then abruptly, in that peculiar way the human mind is sometimes known to function, the solution to the enigma of Rojas' death struck Bucher with the effect of a bucket of ice water thrown in the face. But of course, dammit! A new element had entered the scene! An unexpected and vigorous and vicious element in the form of Rojas' murderers. These killers had been waiting in Rojas' office, even as Bucher was whaling the tar out of the man—all of which posed another urgent question: Who was this new element? What was their number and whom did they represent? The Syndicate? Hardly, Bucher thought. Not the main body of the Syndicate, headquartered in the United States. Hernán Gris was affiliated with the Syndicate, in a manner of speaking, but loosely, the same as el Roca was in Matamoros, but why would the Syndicate want to involve itself with things of questionable value, such as Dr. von Kessler's $H(g)A-7$? Of course, there was Nick Ferroni. Ferroni was in the Syndicate, solidly in, but in this particular instance Bucher was willing to wager his last dime that Ferroni, whatever his interests in von Kessler and $H(g)A-7$, was functioning as an independent, without Syndicate sanction. And probably without Syndicate knowledge.

Aside from all this, whoever had ordered Rojas' death and done the man in had tremendous influence with the local police. This much was undeniable. Not only had the police failed to investigate any of the goings-on at the Diablo, but apparently word had spread and everyone now shunned the place.

"Bucher, we're not going to sit here all night, are we?" Isabella asked quietly in the darkness of the Land Rover's cab.

Bucher was about to reply when the peaceful hush of the tropical night was destroyed by a piercing, feminine scream of watery-gut terror, the sound coming from a point they could not see farther along the poorly lit street. At the same instant that Bucher made out the figure of a woman fleeing in the gloom toward the Land Rover, a violent, terrified scream shattered the dark silence a second time. Bucher reacted automatically.

"Get her inside the truck," he snapped to Isabella as he rolled from the cab. So many cockeyed, woefully screwed up things were taking place lately that it never occurred to Bucher that the fleeing woman might not be connected with the problems facing him, for instinct told him otherwise.

Isabella's reaction was no less quick than Bucher's. In fact, when the strange woman fell to her knees in front of the Land Rover, pleading hysterically for help, Isabella reached her first because Bucher's attention was focused back down the street in the direction the woman had come from, searching for anyone in pursuit. He saw no one and, seconds later, between them, they hustled the terrified woman into the vehicle. Bucher lost no time in backing out of the side street and speeding off, searching through his memory for the basics of the crude map Señorita Delosa had given him when she had suggested that he and Isabella spend the night at the small house the map was drawn to direct them to. Earlier the house had offered little attraction; at present it offered very much attraction, indeed, and since el Roca used it as a sanctuary during his visits to San Luis Potosi, it would be well protected and easily defended.

Isabella, with many soothing reassurances to their unexpected passenger, had the woman calmed by the time they had reached their destination and Bucher had concealed the Land Rover among the lime trees behind the building. Bucher unlocked the rear door, and Isabella led the woman inside, the two women talking in quiet voices in the main room while Bucher checked the security of the house.

It was small but lavishly furnished; in keeping with el Roca's tastes as Bucher remembered them. The doors were of heavy, metal-reinforced timbers, and the windows were covered with thick iron bars. Considering the two-foot thick adobe walls, it would take an experienced bomb squad to break into the place at all, and to do so without alerting any occupants inside would be impossible. Satisfied, Bucher returned to Isabella and the other woman in the main room, the latter adjusting her disarrayed garments as he entered.

The instant his eyes fell on the woman, he knew he had seen her before. On his first visit to the Diablo earlier in the evening it was she who had directed him to Pablo Rojas. He took a seat on the side of the room opposite the rattan couch where Isabella sat. The woman sat down beside her.

"What's your name?" Bucher asked without preamble.

"María Rosa Belén," Isabella replied for the other, "and on her mother's side of the family she is the niece of Hernán Gris."

On hearing this bit of unexpected information, Bucher stared fixedly at María Belén for half a dozen heartbeats, his expressionless face revealing nothing of the fierce exultation suddenly charging through his big frame. He had been right! Before rescuing her back in the side street, his instinct had informed him she was connected, however remotely, with the problems at hand. That she was now with them in this place was an incomparable gift of Lady Luck. Now, dammit! Perhaps he would learn something that could serve as a foothold to help him solve the enigmatic group of circumstances and events he thought of as the von Kessler caper.

María Belén was an inch or so taller than Isabella, also a few pounds heavier, which gave her that lush, voluptuous figure men of Latin blood find so captivating. But otherwise her features bore no distinctive characteristics; she was typically Mexican, a young woman of perhaps twenty who could easily have vanished in any crowd of Mexican women of her own age group.

"Why did you work at the Diablo?" Bucher asked her in Spanish. "To report on Rojas' activities to your uncle?"

María nodded mutely, then: "I am acquainted to a degree with Rojas' affairs; whom he saw, what he did, and if anything out of the ordinary occurred I was to dispatch a message to my uncle at once."

"How do you get your reports to Ajo?"

"Through the mountains on horseback Ajo is only three or four kilometers from San Luis Potosi. My uncle owns a small corral on the outskirts of the city. Some of his Indian employees are always there to carry the messages. I was on my way to this corral when I discovered that the two men who had killed Pablo Rojas were pursuing me. I became sick with fear, for they kept getting closer and closer and I could in no way evade them—until I screamed and fled down the street where you and Isabella rescued me."

Bucher tried to hide his incredulity, but it showed in his tone. "You know who killed Pablo Rojas?"

"I saw them do it!" María shuddered. "It was—ghastly." She took a deep breath, got tighter control of herself and continued, looking directly at Bucher. "When you beat Rojas, broke all the bottled drinks behind the bar and left, Rojas staggered into his office, and I went into a small storeroom, thinking to get fresh drink for any of the customers who wanted it. The storeroom has two doors, one opening onto the main section of the cantina and through which I entered, and another connecting the storeroom with Rojas' office. I was in the storeroom when the two men killed Rojas, or began killing him—" she shuddered again "—for it took some time. Anyway, I crept out the same door I had entered and told all those present in the cantina to flee. I fled also. Somehow the killers learned of my witnessing their crime and came after me."

"Who are the two men?" Bucher asked tersely.

"I do not know Señor."

"You just told me you saw them."

"Yes, and heard them talk, but I had never seen them before, and they spoke very poor Spanish; Spanish such as a tourist might learn from a textbook. Therefore Spanish is not their native tongue."

"Could you identify their nationality through any conversation they had with Rojas?"

"I speak only Mexican-Spanish, Señor, and a little Indian. In their tourist-textbook Spanish they apologized profusely to Rojas in a sadistic, macabre manner for the need to kill him, but explained that orders were

100

orders and Number One had decreed that he must die because he was in the way, and this Number One person was taking over the entire operation of something; I do not know what. Then one of them got behind the chair to which Rojas was tied, placed the thong about his neck and began killing him. At this point the other one was busy explaining to Rojas that Number One would avenge the beating you gave him, because this Number One intended to kill you in person."

"One of the killers said that about me?"

María nodded. "You are the one who is called the Butcher, no?"

Bucher nodded bleakly, concealing his dismay. Carlos Rodríguez, shortly before he died, also had said this person referred to only as Number One harbored a strong desire to kill him personally. Try as he would, Bucher could recall no one in the Syndicate nicknamed Number One; nor out of the Syndicate either, for that matter.

"María," he asked suddenly, "what language do the Nahuatl Indians speak?"

"Aztec-Mayan, and usually it is sprinkled with a few Spanish words unless talking to another Indian."

"Why do you ask?" Isabella said suspiciously to Bucher.

He ignored her question. "And where is this corral belonging to your uncle, where Gris' Indian messengers hang out?"

"On the outskirts of the city on the highway leading to Saltillo. One cannot miss it."

"Good girl." Bucher rose to his feet. "I'll act as your bodyguard, and you take a message to be delivered to your uncle."

Bucher did not like making the trip with two women whom he felt he must protect, but Isabella gave him no alternative. Fortunately, a fat, silvery moon hung high in the Mexican sky as they neared their destination.

CHAPTER NINE

"How many Nahuatl Indians are we likely to find at the corral?" Bucher asked María, wheeling the Land Rover off the main highway to Saltillo and onto a dirt road.

"No more than two men and the woman who cooks their meals. What message do I give them, Señor?"

"That Number One's assassins have killed Pablo Rojas and intend to kill your uncle, because Number One intends to take over control of his entire operation."

Bucher had no way of knowing whether he told the truth, aside from the part about Rojas' death, but the story would draw Gris' attention away from Bucher long enough for him to get a clearer picture of what was going on. And God, did he ever need a clearer picture!

Thanks to the full moon and the clear air of the high altitude, visibility was very good, and as Bucher braked the Land Rover to a halt at the corral that loomed out of the darkness, he saw it contained three horses and was adjacent to a small, flat-topped adobe building. At one corner of the building an Indian woman sat on her haunches shaping tortillas and baking them on a flat rock over a charcoal fire. Two

Indian men, also on their haunches, squatted one on either side of the building's single door. All three rose to their feet when the Land Rover stopped moving, and stood looking at it in stolid curiosity in the bright glare of the vehicle's headlights.

"Keep the lights on and the motor running," Bucher told Isabella as he and María dismounted from the cab. "I'll accompany María."

He had an ulterior motive in this. Mexico has several dozen different dialects, but all find their origin in the ancient Mayan language, which Bucher spoke fluently, and he wanted to hear the Nahuatl Indians speak, in order to learn if he could communicate with them by talking to them. His facility with languages other than his own had stood him in good stead in the past, and it might again.

"Señora, Señores." María, speaking in Spanish, inclined her head in a polite nod of greeting with each word. "I have a message for my uncle, Hernán Gris." Then she rattled off a mixture of Spanish and Indian that Bucher had little difficulty in following, repeating the story he had told her to send to Gris. When she finished, one of the men, who spoke in guttural, gravel-crusher tones, asked her in halting Spanish to repeat the message, but for the sake of clarity this time speak more slowly. Part way through her second delivery the man gestured impatiently with head and hand, indicating he still did not understand all she said.

"Some of them understand hardly any Spanish at all," María said in a brief aside to Bucher.

"Let me try," he said quietly. He then repeated her exact words, but in the ancient Mayan language, and when he finished, the three Nahuatls stared at him in wonder.

"My name is Ixchotl," said the rough-voiced man María had been trying to talk with. "Who is this stranger who speaks the Nahuatls' mother tongue as if he has been born among us?"

"My English name is Bucher, friend Ixchotl," Bucher replied, then lied boldly. "My other name is Zaxatkn; son of the Mayan Indian princess Melotzn from near Chetumal in Quintana Roo, many days to the south of here."

"You're a lying son of a bitch!" a masculine voice snarled in English from the dark interior of the adobe hut.

Bucher stiffened almost imperceptibly, but gave no other evidence of surprise at hearing Nick Ferroni's greasy voice. A second later Ferroni emerged into the light, in his hands a deadly twelve-gauge, semi-automatic shotgun.

"Hello, Nick, ol' buddy," Bucher said softly, mental picture of Mary Waites' body flashing before his mind's eye.

"I don't know much, but I've picked up enough Mex from these greaser Indian bastards to know you're lying; just you saying it makes it a lie. And don't make any false moves, Butcher-boy. Nor that dame with you either. I got six loads of double-0 buckshot in this shoulder cannon, so don't neither of you try anything funny. Understand?"

"I understand."

"Then get your goddamn hands in the air!" Ferroni spat. "Both of you!"

"Raise your hands, María," Bucher said in Spanish from the side of his mouth, eyes on Ferroni and wondering what was wrong with the man. "Otherwise he might kill us."

María's hands shot straight up as she loosed a tiny whimper of terror.

"Now." Ferroni licked his lips nervously. "Now tell me in English about that message you've got for Hernán Gris."

Beginning to suspect that Ferroni's bravado was a weak façade, and seeing no purpose to be served in not doing so, Bucher told him the message with numerous embellishments for added effect, and even as he gave the account of Pablo Rojas' gruesome death, he sensed a very decided change come over Ferroni, a change that reeked of the man's fear-sweat.

"And so," Bucher concluded, alert for an opportunity that would not endanger the life of the young woman beside him, "if this mysterious Number One joker is taking over the whole territory down here, you're probably on his rub-out list also."

"That's a lie." But this time Ferroni's snarl was a flimsy sound of uncertainty. "Number One wouldn't pull a stunt like that." This was more of a question than a statement.

"Why don't you ask Pablo Rojas if Number One would or wouldn't."

"A couple of Gris' boys are working with me and are due here any minute. I'll check with them."

At this, Bucher realized Ferroni was ignorant of the fate that had befallen Carlos Rodríguez and Gustavo Sánchez. "If you're expecting Rodríguez and Sánchez to make the scene, don't hold your breath." He paused for effect, then continued, lying. "Number One got them same as he did Rojas."

Ferroni's bravado now sagged badly. "H-How did you learn that?"

"I came across their bodies at a small cluster of

'dobe huts about twenty kilometers north of San Luis Potosi."

The stink of Ferroni's fear-sweat grew noticeably stronger, confirming Bucher's conviction that Number One was a fiend in human form, for the Nick Ferroni that he knew didn't scare easily. Yet the mere suggestion that Ferroni's name might be on Number One's rub-out list had dissolved Ferroni's courage in short order. Bucher decided to exploit the man's fear to the limit.

"You want to make a deal, Nick, ol' buddy-roo?"

"Hell, no." Yet Ferroni's fear was suddenly joined by cautious hope. "What sort of a deal? What's my cut?"

Bucher felt like shouting for joy. Lowering his arms, Bucher said in Spanish to María, "Go wait for me in the car," repeating it in English for Ferroni's benefit.

"Okay, okay," Ferroni said grudgingly. "I asked you what sort of a deal. What's my cut?"

"I'll guarantee you'll escape Number One's rub-out list in exchange for information." Bucher held his breath, hoping against hope Ferroni would take the bait, but knowing that whether he took it or not, he, Bucher, was going to avenge Mary Waites' brutal murder before the hour was out.

A long, silent minute passed before Ferroni spoke again, but during that minute the muzzle of the shotgun in his hands slowly eased six inches lower, out of line. Under other circumstances Bucher would have burned him on the spot, but not now. Not with Ferroni a possible source of answers for questions that had been nagging at him.

"What sort of information do you want?" Ferroni asked at last, then added quickly before Bucher could reply, "Wait a minute! Have I got your word I'll escape Number One's rub-out list?" Even when the Butcher was still in the Syndicate, his given word was to be trusted more than the Federal Reserve System.

"You've got my word that you'll never make it with Number One's rub-out list," Bucher told him confidently. "I promise." And it was a promise Bucher meant to keep or die trying.

"Okay." Ferroni relaxed visibly. "That's good enough for me. What sort of information do you want?"

"Who is Number One? What's his nationality? What's his interest in Dr. Bruno von Kessler's H(g)-A-7?"

Again there was a long silence, then Ferroni said:

"Number One is the code name of Jules Lurante. He's a Frenchman, kingpin of the Paris rackets. He wants the H(g)A-7 so's he can use it against the United States, to bring the country to it's knees so's he can sell it state by state to the highest bidder. It sounds crazier'n hell to hear it said, but he can do it on account of H(g)A-7 isn't a tranquilizing gas like von Kessler claims. That's only the initial effect when the gas evaporates and is first breathed. It tranquilizes then, but at some point between the second and third week after breathing the stuff the one who's breathed it goes mad."

Even though this was no news to Bucher, but just confirmation of a conviction, it caused a hard, cold lump to form in the pit of his stomach. Even so, he did not permit his emotions to be reflected in his voice.

"What's Hernán Gris' part in the set-up?" he asked quietly.

"Gris is Number One's—Lurante's—flunky in Mexico, nothing more. I knew Gris from a long time ago, and bringing von Kessler to Mexico was easier than taking him to France. Lurante wanted von Kessler on hand until he made certain von Kessler's $H(g)A$-7 is what it is; that it makes people who breathe it go mad instead of only tranquilizing them for a while."

"Where is von Kessler now?"

"With Gris as far as I know. Here in San Luis Potosi."

Bucher exerted conscious effort to prevent revealing his surprise. "Where in San Luis Potosi?"

"In an old, abandoned silver mine. It's called the mine of the Fallen Angels. It's been out of commission for over a century so far as silver mining goes, but Gris has it all fixed up inside as a supersecret hideout, just in case."

"Who else knows of this supersecret hideout, Nick? Does Lurante know?"

"He sure as hell does. Von Kessler is there. I passed the location of the hideout along to Lurante when I took a can of film to him in Paris."

"A film of an experiment with $H(g)A$-7 on five Mexicans in a small adobe room?"

"How the hell did you learn about that?" Ferroni demanded suspiciously. "Rodríguez and Sánchez had the only other print of that film. And where's the von Kessler chick, by the way?" The suspicion was replaced by the greasy chortle that edged into Ferroni's voice. "Man, did I have plans for that chick. Been too long already since I got me some real good jollies."

Revulsion surged through Bucher, and he hesitated before speaking again, searching his thoughts for other important questions that were vitally in need of answers. He found none. Somehow the knowledge of who had marked him for the rub-out twice in Paris had lost its attraction—he was virtually certain Jules Lurante, as Number One, was behind the tries anyway. A number of other things also had lost their value in light of the surprising information given him by Ferroni. Imperceptibly Bucher gathered his muscles; it was now time to surprise his informant.

"Isabella von Kessler is with me," he said with a movement of his head. "There in the Land Rover. We've got the spare copy of that film. I took it off Rodríguez and Sánchez after I burned the bastards."

Ferroni started violently, as if stabbed from behind by a white-hot needle. *"You* burned 'em?" he shouted. "You said—"

"I lied," Bucher snarled.

"You lied?" Ferroni screeched. "We got a deal! You promised to get me off Lurante's rub-out list! Was that a lie?"

"No!" Bucher's voice was flat, cold.

Ferroni sniggered impulsively in massive, instant relief. The Butcher never broke his given word.

"I promised you'd be dropped from Lurante's rub-out list," Bucher said.

"Then let's get the hell out of this place!"

"No dice, Ferroni!" Bucher's voice cracked like the lash of a bull whip. "You escape Number One, but not me. Remember that little Mary Waites you got your jollies from in Pittsburgh a few years ago? You've got to answer for her death, Ferroni. To me. *Now!"*

The shotgun in Ferroni's hands started to come back into line on Bucher.

"Koosh!" The silencered P-38 that appeared in Bucher's big mitt sighed gently.

The shotgun fell from Ferroni's hands to the ground

without firing as Ferroni screamed insanely and grabbed his crotch with both hands, blood from his shattered genitalia spurting through his fingers. He staggered backward a step to come up against the adobe wall near the Indian named Ixchotl. Ixchotl stepped away contemptuously, and Ferroni lurched up in an attempt to go for the shotgun.

"*Koosh!*" Again the Walther in Bucher's hand sighed gently, its nine millimeter slug striking an inch above Ferroni's pelvic bone. It tore through his lower intestine and blasted out his lower back, barely missing the bone.

And Ferroni screamed, and he screamed, and he screamed raw, blistering screams of mortal agony, screams that soon gurgled with blood from ruptured veins in his throat.

Bucher, remembering, never moved until Ferroni died. It took Ferroni five minutes. It had taken Mary Waites over an hour. When silence fell, Bucher leathered his piece and spoke to Ixchotl in Mayan.

"Are you and your people loyal to Hernán Gris?"

Ixchotl replied without hesitation. "Many of us are in his employ, but by necessity, not by choice. Hernán Gris is an evil man."

"He is of your blood."

"He claims to be of our blood, and we pretend to believe it; again from necessity."

"I need your assistance," Bucher said frankly. "And will pay well for it, yet I might be an evil man also."

Ixchotl eyed the corpse of Ferroni, which lay near him, then spat on it. "To kill such a vile one as that, you cannot be evil. We know how he uses women. What assistance do you need from us, Zaxatkn?"

For a second the question caught Bucher a mite off

balance; until he remembered having told the Nahuatls his mother was Mayan and his Indian name was Zaxatkn. He dug a wad of hundred dollar bills from his money belt and handed them to the man. The other Indian man and the woman had gathered closer to hear the conversation, and when they saw the denomination of the bills, they gave forth murmured exclamations of surprise and pleasure.

"Do you know where the old abandoned silver mine, the one called the mine of the Fallen Angels, is located?" Bucher asked.

"We know. It was our ancestors who named it the Fallen Angels. Many of them died in it under the early Spaniards. What are your wishes regarding this mine, Zaxatkn?"

"Find Gris' secret entrance to the place and post men to watch it. I want to know who enters, who leaves, and where they go. Can you manage it?"

Ixchotl nodded. "With great ease. My people today also worked in the mine for Hernán Gris. Not to dig for silver, but to prepare the great underground living quarters for him should he ever find need to use it. Among the Nahuatls the mine today is no more a secret than it was under the Spaniards of long ago." He turned to the man beside him. "Saddle the horses and hasten to Ajo. Return with enough men to do as Zaxatkn requires. I will wait here; then we will go to the mine." An ominous note entered his tone. "We Nahuatls owe Hernán Gris much, and Fortune has smiled up on us. The time has come to pay the debt."

CHAPTER TEN

Ten minutes later Bucher turned to Isabella who was driving the Land Rover on the way back to San Luis Potosi.

"Pull over to the side of the road and stop," he said sharply.

"Why?" Isabella asked in a strained voice.

"Because I need a goddamn drink, that's why!"

He drank long and deep from the bottle of tequila María found for him in back, drank until he felt his stomach on the edge of revolt.

"Bucher," Isabella asked in a little-girl voice when he lowered the bottle. "Who was Mary Waites? How did Ferroni kill her?"

Only because of the tequila did Bucher feel he was able to discuss the subject. "Ferroni was a garrote artist same as the bastards who killed Rojas, but with a difference. Concerning women and sex. The only way he could feel like a man was to garrote a woman during the act. One of Ferroni's favorite brags to Syndicate cronies was that he always spent an hour or longer getting his jollies. That means it took his victims that long to die."

They were speaking in Spanish and María, incredulous, asked: "This Ferroni—he garroted his victims slowly? To prolong the sex act? Finally killing them at the end?"

"Right!" Bucher snapped. "Now shut up and let's get to the Hotel Anahuac. I need to have another chat with Señorita Delosa."

Isabella and María obeyed. They shut up. But the revelation of Ferroni's fiendish hang-up had so shaken them that each took a big drink from Bucher's bottle before the Land Rover was back on the road again.

They found Señorita Delosa at the Anahuac, still behind her desk though no longer on duty. She lay on the floor behind the desk, bound hand and foot, eyes bloodshot and bulging, purpling tongue protruding, the garrote that had been used to murder her buried in the soft flesh of her throat. She had been dead only a few scant minutes when they found her. Pinned to the top of her dress was a note written in a fine spidery hand that, in English, read: "Thus will soon the dread Butcher die, and very, very soon."

Bucher swore a string of blistering oaths. Señorita Delosa's death all but proved something that he had, only within the past few hours, grown to strongly suspect. Lurante, as Number One, was somehow, in some way, by some means, learning of his every move before he made it! Lurante had known he was returning to the Diablo, and Pablo Rojas had died. Lurante had known he was going to the Gris corral, and his arch enemy, Nick Ferroni, had been waiting with a shotgun. Lurante had known he was returning to the Anahuac, and Señorita Delosa had died. It was un-believable, even uncanny. Nevertheless it was the very truth. Bucher felt it in his bones. Yet how the *hell* was it humanly possible for Lurante to learn of his moves beforehand?

"What did you want to see Señorita Delosa about, Bucher?" an ashen-faced Isabella whispered.

"I need to contact some people in the states at once," Bucher replied absently, his thoughts on Lurante. "With both the telegraph and the telephone systems in San Luis Potosi shut down for the night, I thought Señorita Delosa might know how—"

"But only the telegraph service is closed down, Señor Bucher," María interrupted quickly. "Not the telephone system. It never closes down any more. That is Mexican law."

When Bucher assimilated the meaning of her words for half a minute he simply stared, mentally staggered. Insane laughter at his own ineptness gathered in his throat. María was right! What she said was true— though once it would not have been—the Mexican telephone service did not cease to function at night anymore. He had been busy with urgent matters when he had found the telegraph office closed on his arrival in San Luis Potosi, and he had assumed, without really giving it any thought, that the phones would be down also.

"Señor," María said, a touch of alarm in her voice. "Such a strange expression on your face."

"Yaah!" Bucher snorted in rank self-disgust. "You'll see the same expression on any man's face the moment he discovers he's been a goddamn fool!" He scooped up the corpse behind the desk into his arms, carried it to one of the rooms lining the hall leading off the lobby, and deposited it onto the bed.

"Bucher," Isabella said when he returned, "María

has relatives living in the same block as the Anahuac. She is going to them."

"You've been a great help, María." The smile he gave the young woman was in reality a reflection of the relief he felt in being rid of her. Instinct told him the nitty-gritty was coming soon, and, in all truth, in a kill-quick-or-die blood-gutsy she would only be extra baggage.

"Now close the hotel door and lock it," Bucher said to Isabella when María was gone. "I've got a phone call to make."

"She's terrified," Isabella mumbled, almost as if speaking to herself. "And I'm not sure her terror isn't more of you than of anyone else. She almost fainted when you shot Ferroni."

Bucher scarcely heard her. He was already busy at the late Señorita Delosa's desk.

It took him twenty minutes to encode the message to White Hat, and less than half that length of time to send it. When it was done, his brow was beaded with sweat and he felt a bit nauseated.

"What is it?" Isabella asked in alarm. "Did you drink too much of the tequila? You look ill."

"I am ill," Bucher growled. "I'm sick as hell with disgust at myself."

The root cause of Bucher's self-disgust lay in the fact that he had failed to determine, until now, the technique whereby Jules Lurante, as Number One, was keeping abreast of his movements, by knowing in advance each move he made even before he made it.

"Listen carefully," he said to Isabella. "We're going to go back outside, get in the Land Rover, and get the hell out of San Luis Potosi. But don't say a word;

116

understand? From now until I tell you it's okay, don't utter one syllable. Not one. Do you understand?"

Isabella nodded, saying nothing.

Some minutes later they cleared the outskirts of San Luis Potosi at seventy-five miles an hour, headed north on Highway 57, in the direction of the mesquite trees beside the small river where they had waited earlier for nightfall. Bucher did not take the turnoff leading to the mesquite trees, but on reaching it halted the vehicle on the edge of the highway. Once again he indicated to Isabella that she was to say nothing, then crawled into the rear of the Land Rover.

Since he knew what he was looking for, he located it in short order, the main components of the equipment in the bottom compartment of a built-in chest of drawers, one set of wires leading to the Land Rover's battery, another set to the radio antenna. Isabella looked on in silent amazement as he ripped the wires loose and piled the components on the floor.

"Okay," Bucher said. "Now we can talk in privacy."

"What on earth is all this about?" a thoroughly puzzled Isabella asked.

"That's a radio transmitting unit; I've been wired for sound ever since el Roca loaned me this heap, and that could mean el Roca is in cahoots with Jules Lurante, though I find it damn hard to believe. Or it could mean some of el Roca's enemies wired the vehicle to keep tabs on him when he used it, and those enemies are in cahoots with Lurante. Which is more probable."

"You mean that all we've said while inside the Land Rover has been monitored?"

"Right. Every sound was monitored."

"Even this afternoon when we woke up . . ." Her words trailed off, her face flushing a deep crimson.

Bucher nodded, beginning to feel good inside—watch out from now on, Number One Jules Lurante sonofabitch.

"Oh, my God!" Isabella's shame and anger were enormous. To have the most precious, most intimate moments of her life the property of total strangers literally stunned her—until Bucher burst out laughing. She struck at him once, though playfully, and then joined in his laughter.

Minutes later they were on their way again, and ten miles further up the road Bucher slowed, shifted to extra low gear and four-wheel drive and cut the lights—and let the Land Rover live up to its reputation of being one of the best off-the-road vehicles in the world. He steered carefully by moonlight as the vehicle, far from any other road, crawled over several miles of rough terrain that had never before seen a motorized vehicle. They finally stopped on the pebble bed of a dry stream in a brush-choked arroya, and Bucher breathed a sight of heartfelt relief. They were safe at last. With the electric monitoring gear disconnected, Lurante could neither overhear their conversations nor get a fix on their position with a direction finder. In the morning Bucher was determined to return to San Luis Potosi, take on Jules Number One Lurante, Hernán Gris, and anyone else who got in his way.

"Where are you going?" Isabella asked quickly as he prepared to leave his seat behind the wheel.

"To throw that monitoring junk out the back and straighten up the place. I need a rest for what's ahead tomorrow.

"You stay here," Isabella said. "I'll do it."

118

While she busied herself in back, Bucher reviewed the events pertaining to the case and soon became aware that his discovery and subsequent destruction of the electronic monitoring equipment brought a sense of relief so intense it felt as if a massive weight had been lifted from his shoulders. His blunder regarding the Mexican telephone system was an incredible stupidity on his part, yet with his message already in the hands of White Hate, even that became trivial now. With the information he had both unearthed and blundered upon in San Luis Potosi, the insurmountable problem of a few hours ago was now hammered down to manageable size. At least here in Mexico. White Hat would lose no time in taking care of the French end of the problem.

Actually, Bucher reflected, his only real remaining problem was to thwart Lurante's plan to spread H(g)A-7 throughout the United States, and he did not believe such an amount of the chemical compound had as yet been manufactured. Regardless, with the information he'd got from Nick Ferroni, and with the aid of Hernán Gris' Nahuatl Indians, tomorrow Number One Lurante was a goner flat out.

The many trivial complexities that still remained unexplained, such as who was behind those two rapid-fire tries to rub him out in Paris, disturbed him not a whit. He felt certain Lurante was behind them, and Lurante was finished tomorrow, so that was that.

Then Bucher found himself recalling with not little pleasure the stunning beauty and titillating charms of none other than Yvette d'Aquitaine. When this von Kessler hassle was over and done with, he just might by god return to Paris for a rendez-vous with Yvette in one of the upstairs bedrooms at Monbrison Health Spa—providing he could get away from Isabella.

"Here, worthless male." Isabella handed him a thick sandwich of Vienna sausage over his shoulder. "And here's a can of beer I found. It isn't cold but it's wet so eat hearty." She threatened him fetchingly with a delightful grimace. "You may need all the strength you can muster for what lies ahead tomorrow."

Because of his immense relief and the good feelings grown better by the moment, Bucher entered into the spirit of her teasing. "Don't tell me I'm in for a hard time."

"Mmmmm, you might say that." The great well-spring of happiness that earlier in the day had begun bubbling inside Isabella now increased swiftly, and in the cramped passageway connecting the front and rear sections of vehicle it bubbled over in girlish laughter, and she hugged herself deliciously in wondrous joy.

The sun was an hour high over the Sierra Madre Oriental Mountains when Bucher, a drowsy Isabella beside him, reentered San Luis Potosi and headed straight for the telegraph office on Calle de Bolívar, where Bucher expected to find waiting a reply from White Hat to his coded phone message of the night before.

The good feelings Bucher enjoyed the previous evening were considerably less in evidence when viewed in the raw realities of the new day. In truth, though he made no mention of the fact, somewhere in the dimmer periphery of his consciousness there lurked a foreboding premonition of evil; a circumstance he dared not ignore. Thus far in the von Kessler case he had accomplished little, and to be further afflicted with additional lacks of accomplishment could spell tragedy.

The small parking area behind the building housing the telegraph office was deserted except for one spotted cur with a battle-torn ear and a pair of indifferent burros.

"Wait for me here in the car," Bucher said to Isabella as he cut the motor. "I'll only be a few minutes."

"Hurry." She gave him a sleepy smile. "I'm starved, and I've about had it with sandwiches. Surely in daylight we can find a restaurant that isn't cluttered with dead bodies or someone wanting to kill you."

Bucher, his thoughts involved with prospects of the day ahead, merely nodded and dismounted from the cab. Last night at the corral, and like a one hundred proof dummy, he had forgotten to set up a meeting point with the Nahuatl Indian, Ixchotl, whom he had hired to stake out Hernán Gris' secret entrance of the Fallen Angels mine. Therefore he must devise some way of locating and contacting the man as soon as he finished at the telegraph office.

The telegraph office had only one attendant on duty, a heavy shouldered young woman with a broad beam, unfettered, pendulous breasts, and a disconcerting mustache, who thumbed unhurriedly through a small stack of telegrams, at last coming across one with Bucher's name on it. In his anxiety to decode the wire on his way to a wooden bench against the wall at the side of the room, Bucher collided solidly with a barefoot boy who had entered the building at his heels, unaware of the lad's covert, speculative stare.

The decoded message contained three distinct parts, which Bucher read swiftly three times, the first in eagerness, the second in astonishment, the third in staggering dismay, especially part three. Part one in-

121

formed Bucher he could expect a second White Hat agent—to serve as his back-up in case he needed one—to arrive in San Luis Potosi at any minute. Part two said White Hat had learned that J. Basil Scorpini and Gimp Rodicco, two of the Syndicate's most capable triggermen, were in Mexico at the request of Nick Ferroni. Part three disclosed that a two-month-old corpse discovered in Paris only the day before had been identified as the remains of one Jules Lurante.

Bucher's mind flatly refused to assimilate the information in this third part of the message at once, and he read the entire message yet a fourth time before he realized the full import of part three's contents. When this happpened he swore silently, viciously in helpless fury. Last night Nick Ferroni had assumed Jules Lurante was the mysterious Number One and he, Bucher, had foolishly accepted that assumption as fact. Yet with Lurante dead two months he could not possibly be Number One—which again raised the maddening question: Who was Number One?

That premonition of impending evil that had been lurking in the outskirts of Bucher's consciousness now seemed much closer, and suddenly he felt naked, exposed, and defenseless, the helpless victim of a thousand eyes watching, waiting, plotting maliciously to entrap and destroy him. To Bucher the feeling was not a familiar one and he cursed again, silently and more viciously than before.

"Señor Bucher?"

Bucher whirled toward the door as he sprang to his feet. The Mexican youth he had bumped into earlier stood looking at him uncertainly.

"Are you Señor Bucher, the Americano?" the boy asked hesitantly.

"Why?" Bucher snarled, and the lad flinched in fear. Common sense plus the self-preservation instinct promptly cautioned Bucher not to let frustration dominate his emotions, and at once he complied, asking the boy civilly: "Why do you want to know if I am Señor Bucher?"

"Because the beautiful lady with green eyes and shiny copper-red hair waiting in the jardin near here promises fifty pesos to anyone who can locate and direct her to the big Americano named Bucher, Señor."

Bucher glanced at the White Hat telegram in his hand. It said for him to expect another agent to serve as his back-up to arrive in San Luis Potosi soon, but surely the back-up would not be Yvette d'Aquitaine. Would it?

It would. And it was. And the instant Bucher's eyes located her seated on a marble bench in the small public garden near a statue of Delores Hidalgo, and despite the tumultuous frustrations engendered by his communication from White Hat, he was smitten by a faint joyful giddiness; until that moment not realizing the impact her dazzling beauty, and Yvette herself, could have on him.

"Well!" she said primly in pretended chagrin as he approach, all the while struggling against a glad smile. "You hide yourself well in Mexico. It took me long enough to find you."

"Get out from behind those sunglasses," Bucher teased, making no attempt to conceal his pleasure. I know who you are. When did you arrive?"

"About an hour ago; I chartered a small plane from Mexico City. You act as if you expected me."

"I got word you were on your way." He sat down beside her on the marble bench.

"And so?" One of her soft hands came over to rest lightly on his.

"And so nothing," Bucher replied grimly. "If you're referring to the case we're on. To put it bluntly, I feel lost." He then proceeded to brief her in detail on his activities since arriving in Mexico, concluding with: "But with Lurante having been dead for weeks, he can't be Number One."

Yvette nodded solemnly, understandingly. "You poor dear. I learned of Lurante's death only an hour or two after you left me in Paris. Raoul phoned me— or was it Pierre?"

"Raoul? Pierre?" Bucher frowned, trying to remember, then succeeded. "Oh, yeah. The two smugglers who think you work for a private detective agency and keep you informed of underworld goings-on."

"For a price," Yvette laughed softly. "I've forgotten which, but one of them called to say Lurante's body had been found."

"I wish," Bucher said dourly, staring absently at the Bureau of Tourist Information sign above a double doorway at a street corner beyond the far side of the jardin, "that we had informants like your Raoul and Pierre here in this burg. Perhaps I could get one of them to tell me what in the hell is going on. I feel that lost; like the dog so confused it chased its—wait a minute!"

Yvette clapped her hands impulsively in delight. "You've thought of something! I knew you would."

"That tourist bureau over there! It'll have a map of San Luis Potosi, showing the location of the Fallen Angels—!"

"Like this?" From her purse Yvette took a folded map of San Luis Potosi, the points of possible tourist

124

interest marked heavily in red. "I stopped at the tourist bureau on my way to the jardin."

"I'll be goddamned," Bucher said dryly in surprise. "Maybe we're going at this whole thing bass-ackwards. Maybe you should take over the case and let me be your back-up."

"Oh—pooh!" Yvette admonished him prettily. Perhaps it's just one of your bad days."

Bucher unfolded the map, surveyed it eagerly. The old original entrance to the Fallen Angels mine, as the crow flies, was less than a mile from where they sat.

"Do you think your Indian friend will be near there?" Yvette asked. "We can be there by cab in a few minutes."

Only then did Bucher remember Isabella in the Land Rover behind the telegraph office. As yet he had said absolutely nothing of her to Yvette, but now he did, relating everything since discovering her bloody and hysterical on the highway except, of course, the two instances of their intimacies, which had no bearing whatsoever on the problems at hand and were the very private property of him and Isabella anyway.

"Oooooh!" Yvette exclaimed in surprise when he finished. "And so the black-haired tart I chased away at Monbrison's is really Dr. von Kessler's daughter. Now vulgar for one to have 'Maverick' tattooed on one's body. And in such a place."

"It's not a tattoo," Bucher growled defensively. "But indelible body paint which she applied herself. Ferroni made her do it on some demented whim."

"Ah-haaaaaa!" Yvette declared triumphantly, teasing. "Now I perceive the reason behind your lack of progress. You have been concentrating on this Isabella's belly instead of the case we're on."

"Saw it off, woman," Bucher grinned, feeling better with each passing minute. The discovery that he had been grossly mistaken concerning the identity of Number One had taken much of the wind out of his sails for a while, but thanks to Yvette's appearance he was recovering fast. "Come on. The three of us will go to the Fallen Angels together. Isabella is waiting in the Land Rover behind the telegraph office."

CHAPTER ELEVEN

Isabella was not waiting in the Land Rover behind the telegraph office. Nor was she anywhere about. The Land Rover was empty. To Bucher's experienced eye Isabella had been taken from the vehicle by force, though clearly she had resisted furiously; on the driver's side of the seat he found several drops of blood.

"What on earth could have happened, Bucher dear?" Yvette asked in dismay.

"Number One has got her," Bucher snarled savagely. "And I'm a damn fool not to have foreseen he would try. The bastard probably kidnapped her in order to use her as a means of forcing her father to cooperate in some way. Get in!"

The Fallen Angels mine had been worked out and left abandoned by the Spaniards over a century ago. At its discovery the entrance of the mine had been well over half a mile from San Luis Potosi, but during the ensuing decades the city had gradually expanded until the entrance, all shoring long since rotted and the tunnel caved in, was now at the edge of the city and would someday be surrounded by it. Few attempts had been made to develop it into a major attraction, only a few sorry-looking signs directed the dedicated tourist to the spot, nothing more.

Bucher parked the Land Rover beside a dilapidated stone building, a cold, sinking feeling of helplessness in his stomach. His coming to the ancient entrance of the Fallen Angels was a futile, empty gesture, and he knew it. In fact, Bucher was tempted to remain in the Land Rover; the entrance, or where the entrance had once been, was nothing but a great concave pocket in the earth, surrounded by slag heaps, all of it now covered with sage, yucca, cacti, and dwarf mesquite.

"It hardly seems worth bothering about," Yvette said drearily.

"Yeah—" Bucher surveyed their surroundings with bleak eyes, "—but since we've come this far . . ." He stepped out of the vehicle, closed the door, and inside his head the world shattered into billions of tiny pinpricks of brilliance as he swirled down and down and forever downward into the bottomless pit unconsciousness.

His return to the world of sight and sound was slow, painfully slow, so slow at times, before reality crystallized completely and as the earth rocked and swayed with him clutching at it to keep from falling off, he was not sure of making it at all. But finally he did, and when at last his senses settled solidly in place, he found himself sprawled face-up, staring dully at a small, dim bulb screwed into a metal ceiling. So, Bucher told himself judiciously, he was in jail, for only jail cells had concrete floors and metal ceilings.

A low, agonized groan reached his ears and he tensed immediately, involuntarily. He was not alone! Without moving his head, Bucher looked in the direction of the groan, and the only thing he could see from his position without moving further was a veined, aged

128

male hand hanging toward the floor from a metal bunk. Still moving nothing but his eyes, he surveyed everything within their reach. It was true. He was in a cell, a cage, for bars were all around, yet instinct told him he was not in a jail in the commonly accepted definition of the word. Yet still in a cell. But a cell *where?*

Gradually Bucher pushed himself up to a sitting position and cast slowly about in all directions. Because of the single, low-wattage bulb, he was unable to see more than a few feet beyond the heavy iron bars surrounding him on all sides, but he could easily see there was only the one cell, occupied by him, and by an old man who lay face up on the bunk, eyes closed, an unruly shock of snow white hair sticking at an odd angle down over his forehead.

Painfully Bucher rose to his feet, stretched hard to unkink muscles grown stiff from having held one position too long, and looked toward the old man on the bunk again. There was something familiar about the old . . . The image on the photograph he had given Señorita Delosa the night before popped into Bucher's mind. Quickly he sat down on the edge of the bunk, took the old man's face in one hand and turned it gently toward the light. Von Kessler! Dr. Bruno von Kessler! Bucher's eyes traveled from the old man's face down over the emaciated body; at various places the garments seemed stuck to the flesh by dried blood, revealing to Bucher that Dr. von Kessler had been brutally beaten, and more than once. Bucher was about to speak when the other opened his eyes; they were old and tired and full of pain and they wandered vaguely in all directions before they at last came to rest on Bucher's grim face.

"Dr. von Kessler." Bucher held his breath, waiting for the other to answer. At long last he did.

"They beat me." The whisper was scarcely audible. "They beat me for hours. Without mercy."

"Dr. von Kessler. My name is Bucher. I came to Mexico to find you and take you back to the states." At this some of the pain went out of the old man's eyes. His interest and attention sharpened noticeably.

"My daughter Isabella," he whispered. "Where is my Isabella?"

"I rescued her from Carlos Rodríguez and Gustavo Sánchez." Bucher did not want to lie to the old man, yet because of his condition, he did not deem it prudent to disclose Isabella's recent disappearance.

"I thank you," von Kessler said in the strongest voice yet, then: "You are here to rescue me also?"

"I am here to try," Bucher said honestly, grimly. "Under the circumstances of the moment, whether I will succeed is a debatable point. Where are we?" His gesture included their surroundings. "Where is this cell located?"

"In one of the storage sections of the Fallen Angels mine. Hernán Gris has—"

"I know." Bucher cut in, not wanting the old fellow to waste his strength in unnecessary conversation. "Where is Gris now?"

"Somewhere in the Fallen Angel, the fiend. He has been here most of the time since I was brought to this place. Gris and two American gangsters named Scorpini and Rodicco tortured me until I gave them the process for producing $H(g)A-7$."

"Are you aware that $H(g)A-7$ produces madness in humans?"

"It does *not!*" the old man retorted with surprising

130

strength. "Only after it is treated with vaporized mercury does it produce madness. But when that happens it is no longer my H(g)A-7, but a different formula altogether, which the deranged mind of Number One calls MM2."

"Who is Number One?" Bucher asked quickly.

"I do not know, unless it is Gris. Or one of the others. I have heard Number One referred to constantly. This Number One is mad, Mr. Bucher. Totally, completely, fiendishly mad."

"How much H(g)A-7 has been produced to date, Dr. von Kessler?"

"To judge from what I have overheard, several thousand gallons. The process is very simple; any junior chemist could do it easily, and Gris has a complete laboratory for doing so farther back in the mine."

"Does Gris have facilities to treat the H(g)A-7 with vaporized mercury also?"

"Naturally. That also is very simple, but only a madman would do it. The mercurized gas, MM2, has an extremely slow deterioration rate and is deadly at a one to one hundred billion ratio. MM2 enters the blood stream through the lungs and soon begins destroying certain brain cells, resulting in hopeless madness."

"Does MM2 have an antidote?"

"No, but it can be neutralized by combining it with equal parts of gasoline. Once it has evaporated there is no stopping or controlling it." Suddenly von Kessler rose to a half-sitting position, eyes staring, a distraught expression on his face. "That is—that is why I say only a madman would produce it." He collapsed back heavily on the bunk and lay still, eyes closed.

Bucher waited a minute to see if the old fellow was

going to speak further. When he decided he was not, Bucher rose to his feet and began silently circling the cell, inspecting each section of the iron bars in search of a means of escape. He found none. He had not expected to. The only way out of the cell was through the door. For whatever reason Gris had constructed a cell in the Fallen Angels, he had constructed a modern one. Even the door had no lock, per se, but was held fast by a metal bolt that was activated by a metal lever sticking up out of the concrete floor eight or ten feet to one side of the cell and impossible to reach—wasn't it?

Seconds later Bucher had stripped to the waist and was tearing his T-shirt into one long strip of cloth four inches wide and long enough, he fervently hoped, to reach the lever. It wasn't. Not with the loop he tied in one end. He started to use his belt for a loop, but instead returned to the bunk where Dr. von Kessler lay; the same as before, with his eyes still closed.

"Dr. von Kessler," Bucher said softly.

The old man neither moved nor gave any sign that he heard Bucher.

"Dr. von Kessler."

Still the old man did not move. Bucher placed a hand over his heart and a moment later realized that the old man would never move again. Bucher swore silently in helpless rage as he removed von Kessler's belt, fastened it into a circle and tied it onto the strip of cloth that had been his undershirt. The bitter-sour taste of defeat was strong in his mouth as he did this, and he did not look at the old man again, feeling that to do so would, somehow, be offensive to them both.

To allay suspicion should anyone appear, Bucher redonned his shirt, empty shoulder rig, and coat. This done, he once again toured the small cell, peering intently through the bars, his eyes better adjusted to the poor light now and trying to pierce the surrounding gloom. Within the past minute or so he had become conscious of the feeling that the cell was situated in a vast, vaulted chamber of the Fallen Angels and located near one of the chamber's walls. The second tour confirmed this feeling. At the rear of the cell he discovered that the sloping side of the chamber was hardly a dozen feet away, and as he continued to stare in that direction, straining to see clearer still, not only did the side of the chamber take on a more distinct form, but so did a number of other objects adjacent to it.

One of these was the body of a man in peon garb that lay stretched out facedown at the base of the wall and, on a shoulder-high shelf built into the wall— Bucher's pulse quickened as he made them out—were his weapons: switchblade, brass knucks, and P-38. As Bucher stood staring through the bars at the body at the base of the wall, an arm of the body moved sluggishly, and the move was followed by a dull sound of pain. Bucher came alert with surprise. He had assumed the man was dead, and on discovering his mistake, impulsively made the universal sound one uses when wanting to surreptitiously attract the attention of another.

"Sssssssssst!"

The sound brought no response from the man against the wall.

"Sssssssssst!"

The figure tensed slowly in an attempt to turn over. The attempt failed, and the figure wilted back into place, this followed by a deep, shaky breath. A full

133

minute passed before the man tried again. This time he made it, rolling over slowly, heavily.

"Ixchotl!" Bucher spoke the name unconsciously in surprise as he recognized the Indian he had hired the night before. Bucher's pulse quickened in excitement. With luck he would not need to bother with lassoing the lever to open the cell door, not if he could get Ixchotl to throw it for him. Then Bucher caught sight of the dark stain discoloring the outside of Ixchotl's trouser leg and the ugly wound an inch or two above the left hipbone.

Little wonder he had initially assumed the man to be dead, Bucher told himself. With a wound like that it was a miracle he was not. Bucher spoke in Mayan.

"Ixchotl, can you hear me?"

"I hear you, Zaxatkn." Ixchotl's tone had lost none of its gravel-crusher qualities, but the voice was so weak it trembled. It took Bucher a moment to remember that Zaxatkn was supposed to be his Indian name. He was about to speak when Ixchotl continued. "As you can see, I was unable to do as you asked. Two of Gris' guards were in the old stone building that concealed the secret entrance to the Fallen Angels."

I'll be goddamned, Bucher said to himself. The old stone building beside which he had parked the Land Rover was the place he had been looking for. Recalling this brought to mind Yvette d'Aquitaine, and alarm touched him. Yet he was not nearly so concerned over Yvette's safety as he was over Isabella's. Yvette's training as a White Hat agent would enable her to take care of herself, but Isabella was no more equipped to deal with the demanding rigors of counterespionage work than a cloistered nun.

"Ixchotl, can you stand?"

134

A long pause ensued, after which Ixchotl answered with a painful grunt as he tried to struggle up to an elbow. "Not yet, Zaxatkn," he said at last. "But my strength is returning. Perhaps soon I shall be able to stand."

Bucher doubted this, seeing how the man was unable even to raise to an elbow, but made no comment regarding the matter, asking instead:

"Do you know how many people are in the Fallen Angels at present?"

"Only Hernán Gris and the foreigners. The foreigners have disposed of all of Gris' men and Gris himself is now their prisoner—I heard the foreigners discussing matters when they thought I was dead. They have built themselves a special chair in which they seat a person and garrote him with great amusement; they are not human."

"What foreigners, Ixchotl?" Bucher asked anxiously.

"That I do not know, friend Zaxatkn, though two of them speak the language I have heard American tourists in San Luis Potosi speak."

Scorpini and Rodicco, Bucher thought bleakly. J. Basil Scorpini and Gimp Rodicco, two of the most bloodthirsty, inhuman killers ever spawned in the Syndicate sewer.

"And you did not recognize the language of the others?" he asked.

"No. It is neither Spanish nor English nor any other civilized tongue I have ever heard."

During this conversation Bucher had been coiling the long strip of cloth with the belt tied to one end in the manner in which a cowboy coils his lariat in preparation for a toss; if Ixchotl could not get to his feet, then for damn certain he would not be able to throw the lever that opened the cell door. Therefore Bucher knew his only chance in getting free was to lasso the lever himself, as he had planned to do originally.

Bucher pressed himself against the bars on the side of the cell nearest the level, prepared to toss his crude lariat, when the sound of distant voices reached his ears. He hesitated, listening intently, and when he realized the voices were approaching, he quickly withdrew and stretched out on the floor of the cell on his side, the lariat under him. He had been in this position perhaps half a minute when lights outside the cell came on, at least two dozen high-wattage bulbs twenty or twenty-five yards apart and forming a circle around the chamber. Bucher squirmed around into a position that permitted him full view of the place and caught his breath in surprise.

The chamber was almost as large as a football field, with the ceiling so high above even the lights did not illuminate it. He was about to conclude that Hernán Gris had spent a sizable fortune on this one chamber alone when he noticed that it had not been formed by the hand of man, but by nature. Gris had only floored the place with cement. In shape the chamber resembled a giant ball that had been cut in half and placed on its flat side; a giant bubble in the earth.

At one end of the chamber a set of stone steps led upward and out of sight, probably up to the old stone house beside which he had parked the Land Rover, and at the other end were great tiers of boxed foodstuffs, jerry cans of gasoline, five gallon carboys of drinking water, and other provisions. At the left extremity of these tiers he saw the mouth of a tunnel, and it was from this tunnel that came the hollow sounds of the approaching voices. He listened carefully.

There was something very much out of the ordinary about those voices! Was it fear? Or was it levity? Or was it a macabre combination of both? Because of distance and their hollow, echoing sound Bucher was as yet unable to distinguish any words, yet as they drew nearer he made out three different speakers— whose tones blended into a mixture of gaiety and watery-gut terror. Suddenly the voices ceased, and when they began again they were much closer. A moment later the speakers emerged from the mouth of the tunnel. There were three men, none of whom Bucher had ever seen before. Two were about thirty-five, clean-cut, short-cropped hair, and exceptionally handsome, with slender but powerful, muscle-padded bodies. They moved with the grace and assurance of superb athletes in the pink of condition, and this in spite of the third man, whom they dragged between them.

This third man was considerably older, nearing sixty by Bucher's estimate, gross-bodied and with a heavy, evil face that was at present blanched in fear. From the two younger men came the sounds of gaiety, from the man they dragged between them the sounds of terror. Bucher frowned in puzzlement, wondering what was going on. He did not wonder long.

At first he thought they were dragging the other to lock him in the cell, though Bucher soon realized that he was much mistaken, and when he recognized the destination of the trio, icy goose bumps covered his body—it was the first time he had noticed the chair.

In certain Latin American countries, and especially in Cuba prior to the advent of Castro's firing squads, capital punishment was carried out by means of the garrote chair, which had been named by some macabre wit la Señorita Silla de Muerte; Miss Chair of Death, or, more briefly, la Señorita Silla. To be sentenced to the clutches of la Señorita Silla was to be condemned to death by a most horrible means indeed, one that caused the most hardened criminals to pale and pray.

The chair itself was constructed of heavy lumber— the one in Cuba's Moncado Prison was made entirely of seasoned oak four-by-fours—and bolted securely to the floor. With the exception of two special features, the chair was merely a straight-backed chair constructed of heavy materials, but these two special features made it an instrument of sadism.

The first of these special features was a five-foot crossbar affixed atop the back of the chair, and along which the condemned's arms were stretched and securely tied at the wrists and elbows. The second was an ingenious metal collar that went around the condemned's neck, and was so constructed that it could be made smaller in circumference by turning a stout butterfly screw in back. This was the executioner's job, to turn this large butterfly screw between thumb and forefinger while a cowled priest stood by doing his mumbo-jumbo act to the grisly sounds of the death struggles coming from the poor bastard tied to the chair.

When Bucher recognized la Señorita Silla, a hot, greasy nausea fermented inside him. The two younger men intended to put the old man to death!

No! Bucher's silent scream of protest went nowhere, had no more effect than would a rubber mallet at trying to dent a thick sheet of carbon steel.

Not only were the two about to garrote the older man, but they were taking immense delight in the atrocity. This was evidenced not only by their actions, but also by their gay banter in high school Spanish—Bucher knew he was looking at the same two killers who had murdered Pablo Rojas and Señorita Delosa. Probably they were two of the sonsofbitches who had bugged the Land Rover and helped thwart every move he had made since arriving in San Luis Potosi. A fierce, deadly rage commenced to smolder inside him.

La Señorita Silla sat near the far side of the chamber, approximately the same distance from the far wall as the cell was from the wall where Ixchotl lay, and the two killers were making so much noise in lashing the old man's arms to the crossbar that Bucher had no fear of being overheard. He twisted around on the cell floor toward the Indian.

"Ixchotl," he whispered harshly. "Can you make it to your feet, man? My weapons are on that shelf above you!"

Ixchotl strove mightily once, twice, thrice to get up off the floor, strove with such intense dedication that great veins swelled and throbbed on his neck, but all to no avail. Once he almost made it to his knees, but pitched back heavily to the concrete with a sharp gasp of pain.

"Saving that man from garroting is a crime in itself," he mumbled thickly and just loud enough for Bucher to hear. "Humanity is better off without Hernán Gris."

Bucher snapped his head around toward the three men at the chair. Hernán Gris? Yes, the old man would be Gris. Killing him would fit the pattern the mysterious Number One had swiftly put into action, gangland style. Killing off everybody that owned a piece of the action was approved Syndicate modus operandi—even though Bucher felt certain the Syndicate, as such, had

139

no part of Number One's scheme against the United States.

Bucher was sorely tempted to try lassoing the lever that would open the cell door, but the lever was in plain view of the killers, and such overt action might catch their attention. If they became aware of his purpose, all hope of his escaping was lost. Fat globules of perspiration dotted his brow, and he felt clammy inside his clothes. Fear was as foreign to his nature as fire is to water, yet he was fully aware of the fact that unless he managed to break free of his confinement, it was only a matter of time before he also became a recipient of la Señorita Silla's deadly embrace. He was not afraid of death; he did not want to die, understandably, yet since reaching the age of accountability he had harbored no illusions that he would live to a ripe old age, his earthly tenure terminating peacefully in bed of natural causes, but to suffer death in a cage at the hands of fiends who derived enormous joy in killing their fellow man . . .

"Anyway, goddammit," he growled savagely to himself. "I'm a long way from dead yet, and before I go down for that last sleep I'll manage to take a few of the bastards with me. Especially Number One."

Some thirty-five or forty yards across the giant bubble under the earth that was a part of Hernán Gris's secret hideout, Hernán Gris was fighting for his very life. And clearly, fighting a losing battle. Gris was almost twice as old as either one of his assailants, and soft and flabby. The two killers were playing with him, neither one putting forth his best efforts to tie Gris' arms to the crossbar, thus prolonging the old man's excruciating fear of death and thereby intensifying their pleasure over the prospects of administering it.

Again hot, greasy bile lurched vigorously in Bucher's stomach. Because of the life style forced on him by an indifferent Fate he was far from unacquainted with the lowest degree of human depravity, yet the inhuman death-drama unfolding before his eyes at the moment shamed him for all mankind. Even though Ixchotl could be one hundred percent correct in saying humanity was better off without Hernán Gris, Bucher knew that if he were not caged like an animal at the moment, he would charge to the old man's rescue.

Bucher studied the two killers with the bleak, merciless stare of the gladiator about to enter the arena. As yet he had heard nothing from them but heavily accented Spanish as they teased and chided and ghoulishly reprimanded the old man for not cooperating with them in his murder. Fear-sweat streamed down Gris' heavy face, and his voice had grown hoarse and wheezy from repeated pleas for mercy. His right arm was now tied fast to the shoulder-high crossbar on the back of the chair, and one of the killers held his left by the wrist easily. Suddenly the other killer, apparently from an uncontrollable surge of emotion, capered completely around the chair in a wildly joyous exultation, coming to a halt in front of it, as he did so saying in clear, concise French:

"Shall we get on with the party, or shall we wait for the arrival of Louise?"

Bucher sat bolt upright in surprise. White Hat's telegram had stated flatly that Jules Lurante was dead! Of course Jules Lurante was not the only underworld boss in . . . And who the hell was Louise? A woman, presumably, since the name was of feminine gender. But it was one of those oddities among names in that it was pronounced, and spelled, exactly the same way in half a dozen different languages in the Western Hemisphere. Inexplicably, a shocking thought thrust itself forcibly into Bucher's mind: Could Louise be Yvette's name also? He shoved the ridiculous thought aside, for a moment having forgotten Yvette was a trusted White Hat agent.

Yet the killer's comment solved for Bucher one irritating enigma. For whatever good or evil it served, he now knew the killers were French.

Hernán Gris, eyes darting wildly from one killer to the other, labored hard for breath, breathing as a man who expects soon to breathe no more.

"Let us proceed with the fun," the second killer said, also in French. "After all, Louise intends to enjoy herself with that Maverick tart and those two pigs in the cell over there; can you imagine receiving a reward of a quarter of a million American dollars for doing in that one called the Butcher?" He turned to the old man seated in the heavy wooden chair. "Come, old one, it is time for the play to commence, and you are the star performer."

For a moment all the fight went out of Hernán Gris, he sagged visibly, seeming to deflate like a punctured balloon, but the next instant he was struggling frenziedly, savagely, against the bonds securing his right arm and the killer's grip on his left, while short, snorty, piglike grunt-squeals of mindless terror issued from his throat.

They tied Gris' left arm to the crossbar with ease, then drew his head back and clamped the metal collar about his throat with even less effort.

Bucher, now sitting propped on one arm, stared in

transfixed horror, knowing they were going to do it but trying not to believe it, fighting internally in order to convince himself it was not going to happen but knowing all the while it was.

CHAPTER TWELVE

Hernán Gris, fast in the unyielding grip of la Señorita Silla de Muerte, had become apoplectic, his body quivering vigorously, his piggish grunt-squeals hoarse and raspy now and interrupted each few seconds by only partially coherent, garbled pleas for mercy.

The killers backed off a step, both grinning hugely as though enjoying their handiwork, and for the first time Bucher noticed how markedly similar they were in appearance. He had seen supposedly identical twins who looked no more alike than they.

"Ahhhh," one killer said to the other with an elaborate bow. "Who has the honor of the first turn of the screw? Do you, brother Raoul, or do I?"

At the sound of the killer's name a sharp, ugly force from within struck Bucher a heavy blow across the midsection, and for half a dozen heartbeats he stared, incredulous, knowing he had heard right but, as before, not wanting to believe. Once more the ridiculous notion concerning Yvette attempted to inveigle its way in among his thoughts, and once again he shunted it roughly aside. In Paris Yvette had said one of the smugglers who kept her posted as to goings-on in the French underworld was named Raoul; the other Pierre, yet this did not mean . . .

"Be my guest," the second killer said grandly, thoroughly enjoying himself. "Never let it be said I let my eagerness to taste the delights at hand render me discourteous. You, dear brother Pierre, get first turn of the butterfly screw."

At this the killers seized each other in a bear hug and did an awkward clog, their gusty guffaws filling the huge chamber as Bucher stared aghast, a trembly sickness taking hold inside him.

Savagely he seized his emotions with his mind, brutally mauled them into subjugation, staggering mentally from the effort but helpless against the insidious, unclean suspicion stealing over him. He shook his head sharply, his thoughts a tangle of contradicting, conflicting pros and cons regarding a possibility he had never before faced, the possibility of a White Hat agent turning traitor to the organization. Such treachery had never happened before in the history of White Hat; this he knew as fact, and if it had happened now, if Yvette d'Aquitaine was indeed a traitor he must—he must . . . Do what? What must he do if Yvette had turned traitor? Kill her? Shoot her down like a mad dog. Involuntarily, mentally, Bucher cringed at the prospect, yet the picture of him killing Yvette had a powerful sobering effect. It straightened out his thinking remarkably. He was not certain he could pull the trigger on Yvette, regardless of the consequences of his not doing so if it became necessary. Anyway, why should he suspect Yvette simply because the two murdering bastards with Gris were named Raoul and Pierre?

"Gugh-gaaaaaak!" This horrendous death rattle

from Hernán Gris snapped Bucher back to the here and now. Raoul stood behind la Señorita Silla pleasantly turning the butterfly screw that tightened the iron collar around Gris' neck, on his face an expression of intense and glorious ecstasy. The hoarse, wheezy sound of Gris' struggle to take just one more breath filled the huge chamber, and Bucher tried to turn his eyes from the doomed old man, clutched again with shame for the human race. Abruptly Gris' wheezing ceased and was followed by noisy gulps; Raoul had backed off on the screw, letting him breathe normally again. The old man was weeping.

Suddenly Pierre turned and trotted across the chamber toward the cell, stopping just beyond arm's reach outside it. Bucher started to get to his feet, then remembered the coil of torn undershirt and Dr. von Kessler's belt, which he still hoped might prove useful in helping him escape, and remained as he was, shielding it with his body.

"Well, well, well!" Pierre cooed chumilly. "What have we here but the great butcher, terror of evildoers and defender of the faith." He sniggered oafishly, continuing primly. "Really, sir, you look like anything but a terror to me."

Bucher studied the man carefully, wondering how the man would shape up in a blood-gutsy hassle. He was big and hard-muscled and powerful, had all the appearances of a go-for-broke fighter, and yet Bucher got the impression Pierre would yellow out if the nitty-gritty got kill-quick-or-die.

When Bucher failed to answer, or even get to his feet, Pierre stepped closer to the bars, peering intently inside—and an icy chill trickled slowly down Bucher's spine when he got a close-up view of the man's eyes.

146

They were fine eyes, widely spaced and a deep, liquid amber, and at first Bucher was hesitant over accepting the conclusion that quickly forced itself upon him. The second scene of the film he and Isabella had looked at yesterday in the mesquite trees beside the small river flickered across his memory; the scene in which the five Mexican peons in the small adobe room had stood staring directly into the camera, insanity, raw and stark, in the eyes of each. That same degree of insanity was now reflected in Pierre's eyes—possibly, Bucher reasoned, from having unknowingly inhaled some of Number One's MM2—and from a wee, far corner of his consciousness it came to Bucher that as a captive of the insane he was much closer to death than at any other time in his entire life. This because the actions of the insane are totally unpredictable. The insane could not be counted on to react as did the sane to any given situation, nor to react the same way twice to the same situation. Again the icy chill trickled down Bucher's spine, but this time he ignored it.

Hard experience had taught him there was no combination of circumstances in life that, with adroit manipulation, could not be milked of an advantage. Perhaps, with luck, he could milk this one. Anyway it was worth a try, for what the hell did he have to lose? Anything to avoid dying like an animal trapped in a cage was worth a try; even playing up to the insane. He forced his features into a childish pout, put a pouty tone to his words, and spoke in French.

"I am not the mean old Butcher either," he said with the proper degree of injured pride. "People just say that about me because they don't like me, darn it. Like that horried Hernán Gris. He's the old meany.

147

He hates me. That's my place in that chair, but old meany Gris won't let me have it because he hates me." He held his breath, fingers mentally crossed.

Pierre gaped at him a full half minute before his handsome face conformed to a boggle of intense glee. He seized himself with both arms and did a frenzied jiggle of delight.

"You really believe Hernán Gris has taken your rightful place in the chair?" he chortled coaxingly.

"I *know* Hernán Gris has taken my place in the chair," Bucher replied, permitting overtones of weedling to creep into his voice. "Can you not move the chair in here so I can sit in it?"

Pierre seemed about to launch into another frenzied dance but did not. Instead he sidled closer to the bars, a crafty lilt in his voice, a look of cunning merging with the madness in his eyes.

"Why don't you come over to the chair instead?" he whispered as Bucher continued to pout, hardly able to believe his ears. "That would be much simpler. I can open this cell door for you if you want. You want to come over to the chair?"

Bucher pretended to ponder the matter weightily. "I don't know," he replied hesitantly at last. "Do you think I should?"

"Of *course,* you should," Pierre gloated. "I'll open the cell door for you." He sprang toward the lever several long steps away.

"Pierre!"

Pierre froze in mid-stride, stopped so abruptly as the sound of his name lashed the chamber that he almost tumbled to the floor.

Something heavy and icy and sickening formed in the pit of Bucher's stomach and a faint giddiness smote

148

him, and it wasn't the sudden destruction of his hopes for freedom that had this effect on him, but his recognition of the voice that had shouted Pierre's name. The voice came from the tunnel through which Raoul and Pierre had earlier dragged Hernán Gris, and when the owner of that voice appeared, something inside Bucher died a little.

Slowly he got to his feet, tossing the coil of torn cloth and belt onto the foot of the bunk where the remains of Dr. Bruno von Kessler lay, and moved to stand close against the bars of the cell. During his brief conversation with the mad Pierre he had been dimly conscious of ugly sounds coming from the direction of la Señorita Silla and now, as he looked in that direction, he saw that Raoul had succumbed to temptation. Gris sat strangely upright in the chair, face bloated and discolored, eyeballs bulging unnaturally, a length of grisly, purplish tongue thrust far out past lips that had frozen in a squirmy contortion after his final breath. Even as Bucher looked, Raoul was busying himself industriously with removing the corpse from the chair. Bucher turned his eyes from the scene toward the person who had emerged from the tunnel and was now approaching the cell.

"So you're the mysterious Number One," Bucher said tiredly, the words sounding as though they came from a great and weary distance. "It occurred to me a time or two that you might be, but I couldn't make myself believe it."

Yvette d'Aquitaine gave him a dainty curtsy and a dazzling smile and, as Pierre had done, stopped in front of the cell beyond arm's reach. The apple green pants suit she wore was in perfect harmony with her emerald green eyes and copper-gold hair and did absolutely nothing to detract from her enchanting beauty.

"You poor boob," she purred throatily. "You never had a chance from the beginning."

Bucher refused to permit any emotion to show on his face, but kept his expression wooden, his eyes and voice flat. "Now that it's too late, I'm beginning to realize that."

She turned from him, addressing Raoul and Pierre, who were lugging Hernán Gris' lifeless body toward the far wall behind the execution chair.

"Raoul. Pierre," she called crisply. "Go bring the other one. I'm curious to see what effect the death of a friend has on the great Butcher." Then again she faced Bucher, continuing at once. "Yes, it is too late. For a moment at the airport in Paris, when you were leaving, my resolution to kill you wavered, but as soon as you left, I got a firm grip on myself once again."

Bucher regarded her in silence, remembering their visit to the health spa; her superbly formed body, the pouting faintly upthrusting breasts plump as honeydew melons ripe to bursting with juice, the flat, satiny expanse of tummy over immaculate thighs, the . . . The thing that but a moment ago in Bucher had died now sprang back to life in the form of cold, murderous hate fraught with rage, neither of which did he allow Yvette to see. But with the bitter-sour taste of defeat strong in his mouth, he gave her instead a smile of grudging admiration, wondering if he could get her to talk, to brag of her exploits. He had never encountered a criminal mastermind who wasn't also an egomaniac under the surface, and even if he was to die for having failed at this caper, he still wanted to know how she had managed to infiltrate White Hat, and if he survived, for damn certain White Hat would want to know, so . . .

"You're pretty good, Yvette," he said, maintaining the smile of grudging admiration. "In fact, and to be perfectly honest, you're the smoothest I've ever seen, and believe me, I have seen some smart ones—or should I call you Louise?"

"How did you learn of Louise?" she asked, a tinge of irritation coloring the words, which revealed to Bucher that she, like all the other great criminals he had come up against, harbored an enormous ego.

"I heard Raoul and Pierre tossing the name about and put two and two together. What beats me, though, is how you managed to hoodwink White Hat."

Yvette smiled easily, completely sure of herself. "That was the simplest thing of all. You have noticed a resemblance between Raoul and Pierre? They are considered to be identical twins, yet there are certain differences between them, both in looks and mannerisms. But if, right this moment, you faced away from me, then turned back and found my twin sister standing here beside me, and we were dressed alike, you could not distinguish which was Yvette and which Louise. Even if you lived in the same house with us for months, or for years, you still could not detect any difference between us." Her smile took on mischievous aspects. "Before his death even my sister's husband could detect no difference between us and he had numerous occasions to do so, though my sister never suspected his infidelity."

Bucher frowned at an imaginary spot at her feet, pretending deep thoughts. "Then you are Louise, eh?" he asked at last. "And your sister is Yvette."

"Was Yvette," she corrected. "Like her husband,

my sister also had a fatal accident one day. So now I am Yvette. Especially to you, dear dumb-boob Bucher, I am Yvette."

Bucher nodded his acceptance. He could not have thought of the woman in front of him as anything but Yvette if he tried.

"What really happened to your sister? I assume she must have been the White Hat agent."

Yvette eyed him curiously. "You really want to know what happened to her, don't you? Why?"

It was time for Bucher to play the trump card that had been lurking anxiously among his thoughts. If her ego was as overbloated as he suspected it was . . .

"Why do I want to know?" he began hesitantly, as if embarrassed to make the forthcoming admission. "Well—let's face facts, Yvette, even though I don't delight in admitting it, you are the very first person on earth to ever get the upper hand of the Butcher. And believe me, a lot of them have tried, so I'm curious to know how you did it, how you fooled me, how you fooled White Hat, the whole shebang." His attempt at a flimsy, deprecatory laugh was highly successful. "Call it a going away present if you like."

Yvette pondered him for a long moment of thoughtful silence, then treated him with another of her dazzling smiles. "Very well, dear dumb-boob Bucher, as your going away present. And Bucher—" a chilling quality crept into her tone, "—you *are* going away. The same as Gris and all others." Without warning the egomania Bucher had therefore only strongly suspected and hoped for surfaced in her face raw and ugly. "And anyway, I think I'm deserving of a few laurels. The successes I've engineered are no mean accomplishments by any definition. I'll tell you what you want to know—for all the good it'll do you. Where shall I begin?"

"At the beginning," Bucher said, trying hard to get a clearer view of her eyes. When they had met in the jardin earlier in the day, and later had driven out to see the original entrance to the Fallen Angels, she had worn dark glasses, but if Pierre was mad from inhaling MM2, then she, and Raoul, might have inhaled some as well.

"The beginning could be when my sister and I were orphaned and separated when we were ten. Her foster parents lived in Paris, mine in St. Reme. We didn't see each other again for eleven years, when I moved to Paris. When we discovered we were so thoroughly identical, what started off as a playful prank soon became our life style. There were some differences between us, though hardly detectable. My sister, I called her Leelee, had a rigid moral code; she believed in flag, country, God, and the like, had immaculate scruples and—well—I believed in living life to my own advantage.

"I had been living in Paris a good while before I discovered a major difference between my sister and me, yet a difference that even Leelee never suspected. She talked in her sleep, at times grew quite articulate. That's how I learned of your precious White Hat." An unclean quality crept into Yvette's tone. "And that's also when I began to lay plans to get all the power and wealth I had always dreamed of possessing. I was already a trained chemist, and with the aid of sleeping pills that I gave her as aspirin, before long I had my sister hooked on heroin without her knowing it. Then I became Yvette, the loyal White Hat flunky, and the real Yvette became Louise, the mainlining junkie who lived from day to day for the fixes I supplied her—until the day the stupid bitch took an overdose. My husbands and I buried her one dark night in a woods outside Paris."

"You and *who* buried her?" Bucher asked in honest surprise.

The shadow of perplexity flickered across Yvette's lovely face, the shadow at once erased by spontaneous, derisive laughter. "You despicable Americans. You're all such prudish holier-than-thous. In reality you have the morals of an alley cat, yet parade yourselves before the world as humanity's God-appointed standard of virtue. Yes, I said my husbands. Raoul and Pierre are my husbands. Does that shock your male chauvinist piggery, dear dumb-boob Bucher?"

Bucher brushed the subject aside, anxious to learn the cause of the madness he had seen in Pierre's eyes. "Have your husbands been helping you treat Dr. von Kessler's H(g)A-7 gas with vaporized mercury?"

Yvette stiffened in surprise, and quick anger mottled her face, which caused Bucher to study her in silent amazement.

"Dr. Bruno von Kessler has flapped his damned lip once too often," she gritted her teeth viciously, advancing a step closer to peer through the bars at the dead scientist on the bunk. "When Raoul and Pierre return they'll give him the full treatment in their chair."

Bucher concealed his surprise behind a poker face, suspecting the reason behind Yvette's lightening-quick reversal of attitude, which reversed itself a second time even more quickly than the first. A soft, glowing smile spread over her countenance.

"But Raoul and Pierre won't give you the full treatment, dear dumb-boob," she purred smoothly. "That is one pleasure I reserve for myself."

"So I gathered from that note you left pinned on Señorita Delosa's body. But why that protective act at the Monbrison Health Spa? Why did you attack Rodríguez and Sánchez? And Isabella von Kessler? And that rescue act later at the Bloody Cat. Were those staged for my benefit?"

Yvette nodded condescendingly. "Right, dear dumb-boob. After all, I only knew the great and fearsome Bucher by his awesome reputation, and I had no way of being certain White Hat did not suspect me of being an impersonator. Did I succeed in convincing you of my authenticity?"

"You succeeded," Bucher said wearily. "You succeeded damn well."

Yvette inched closer still and again peered through the bars at the remains of von Kessler on the bunk. "Is the old goat asleep?"

"The old goat is dead," Bucher said acidly, squelching an impulse to seize her and break her damn neck. As he saw it, doing so would only worsen his plight, not help it. He must first get free of this cage before he could chance going into action.

"Hmmmmm," Yvette mused as though addressing herself. "He was a stubborn old goat though, but I guess they beat him too hard." Again she flashed Bucher her dazzling smile—and he saw the madness glaring at him boldly from the depths of her emerald green eyes. "Those husbands of mine can be rough at times."

My god, Bucher thought, she's no more sane than Pierre, or any of the five peons in the small adobe room. The sensation of slimy worms squirming through his insides beset him. And if Yvette and Pierre were mad, Raoul was probably mad also. Bucher's situation was desperate enough if all were sane, but with them mad . . . Sweat broke out all over his big frame, he felt clammy inside his clothes, and again he acknowledged to himself that never in his life had he been closer to death. Unless he got out of this cursed cell all was lost—if it wasn't lost already. Best he keep Yvette talking as long as possible.

"What is this ridiculous thing Nick Ferroni told me about you hoping to bring the United States to its knees?" he asked conversationally.

"You think it's ridiculous?" Yvette laughed throatily. "I'll bet before you knew it had been done, you'd have said bugging your Land Rover was ridiculous, wouldn't you? Or me bribing the telegraph operator to give you that fake White Hat telegram this morning, or me killing Jules Lurante myself when he was through serving his purpose, or Raoul and Pierre abducting that simpering von Kessler tart while I detained you in the jardin. I'll bet you'd have thought all those things ridiculous, dear dumb-boob." Rank disgust and loathing flavored her next words. "You Americans, you are so revoltingly naive." Positive overtones joined the disgust and loathing. "And you, dumb-boob, are you so simpleminded as to assume my plan for your sacred land-of-God-America is a spur of the moment thing. Believe me, it isn't. The plan has been on the drawing board, you might say, for years, and I was ready to put it into action months ago, but I couldn't discover a host chemical compound that would accommodate my vaporized mercury formula. Then I read of von Kessler's $H(g)A-7$ in that science magazine. I knew it was the host compound

I'd been searching for, only the magazine did not give the process for producing H(g)A-7. I was already doing business in narcotics with Nick Ferroni, whom I met through Jules Lurante, so when I read von Kessler's article I simply promised Ferroni a piece of the action in return for his kidnapping von Kessler and delivering him to Hernán Gris, whom I also had met through Lurante. You know the rest. Or should.

"The moment we got the von Kessler process I produced a batch of my MM2, then wired the manufacturing details to a small lab in Detroit, Michigan, that I own through a front, and right this minute there is enough of my MM2 in every city of over a million population in your precious land-of-God U.S.A. to destroy the sanity of every person in it."

She took a small black notebook from the pocket of her jacket and waggled it at him gloatingly. "It's all right in here: names, addresses, the cities in which my MM2 gas is hidden, and where, everything. And in case you don't know it already, the insanity caused by breathing MM2 is incurable."

Bucher wanted to gag; only by conscious effort did he manage to conceal his revulsion. "And you produced some of your MM2 here in Gris' laboratory?" he asked after a moment.

"My husbands and I produced enough to test it on five peons, then we returned to Paris. Ferroni brought us a film of the experiment." Evil laughter bubbled from her lips. "Ooooooh, you dumb-boob you! Introducing you to la Señorita de Muerte is going to give me such great pleasure. You're so—so exposed, so childish. It's really a simple matter to know what's going on in that law and order brain of yours. You're wondering if Raoul, Pierre, and I wore protective gear when producing my MM2, aren't you? Tell me, aren't you?"

"It crossed my mind."

"Well stop wondering, dumb-boob. We wore gas masks. All three of us. So there!"

"Yeah." Bucher nodded. "That's right." He wondered also if he should tell her a gas mask was no protection against von Kessler's $H(g)A-7$, and apparently none against her MM2 as well. He decided against mentioning it. It was impossible to convince an insane person of his insanity. "So you're going to bring the United States to its knees, eh?" he said, playing for time and hoping for he wasn't sure what to happen. "Where will you begin?"

"The island of Manhattan," she replied promptly, smugly. "With the Federal Reserve Building. Did you know it sits on top of forty billion dollars in gold bullion?" She repeated the words, savoring them, rolling them around on her tongue. "Forty billion dollars. Think of it. Forty billion dollars. And two weeks from now all forty billion will be mine."

For the hell of it Bucher said, "That's only a few hundred thousand tons. You can carry that much in your purse." The words were hardly out of his mouth before he realized it was a mistake to have uttered them. Purely by freak chance, and by freak chance alone, he had touched on a subject that, inexplicably, perhaps because of her mental condition, Yvette had heretofore failed to consider.

Yvette's face flamed the deep scarlet of hate plus rage, and her insane eyes flashed fire. "You son of a bitch!" she screamed at the top of her lungs. "You goddamn no-good law and order son of a bitch!"

Involuntarily Bucher flinched from the force and

violence of her fury. Again the madness was all too plain in her green eyes, not lurking in their depths but boldly on the surface. Her teeth were displayed by drawn-back lips, and at the height of her seizure once, twice, three times she raked the empty air with claw-shaped hands. Then as quickly as it had arrived the seizure fled, and though stone-faced, Bucher stared at her in rank astonishment. Swiftly her color returned to normal, and yet again she treated Bucher to one of her dazzling smiles.

"You rascal," she pouted fetchingly. "You're trying to get me upset."

"I was only teasing," Bucher said in tones of deepest apology, on the spur of the moment deciding to risk another display of her dementia. "Forty billion in gold bullion can't weigh more than a few ounces, especially at today's inflated prices."

"That's exactly the way I have it figured," Yvette replied judiciously. "Transferring it will be no problem at all." She was about to speak further but instead paused, holding up one hand, then continuing joyfully: "Ooooo, I think I hear Raoul and Pierre coming back with the next treat for la Señorita de Muerte. The gleeful exuberance in her voice sent tiny squiggles of horror wriggling all over Bucher.

He had been too busy talking to Pierre, thankfully, to see Hernán Gris meet his end, but something told him he would not be as fortunate this time, and wondered which poor devil was being dragged down the tunnel. He did not wonder long.

Isabella!

Raoul and Pierre dragged her small form between them as they had earlier dragged Hernán Gris, but with much less resistance because she was in much worse shape than Gris had been. Even from his distance Bucher could see that she had been brutally mistreated; her garments were in tatters, her lips swollen, puffy, and there were huge deep-purple circles around both eyes. Also the small wound in her temple that Bucher had closed with adhesive the day before was bleeding again. Bucher cursed himself in impotent fury, feeling himself responsible for her molestation.

"Your husbands have jumped the fence into another barn lot," he gritted savagely.

"So?" Yvette replied archly. "No horse likes the same old stable all the time, nor the stable the same old horse." Her next utterance was an ugly, unwholesome sound steeped in loathing. "Americans," she spat viciously, "naive, simple, stupid."

The two maniacs dragging Isabella were halfway to the death chair when movement behind them, in the direction of the tunnel's mouth, caught Bucher's attention. He did a quick double-take at the sight of the two newcomers, then stared in surprise, mouth and throat parched, hands clammy and sticky with cold. Quickly he seized his emotions, and, by sheer force of will alone, dominated the icy fear seeking to clutch him. At that moment Yvette's back was turned, and he was indeed grateful she did not witness his reaction to the new arrivals.

One of these new arrivals was J. Basil Scorpini, a Sicilian-English half-breed in whom were combined all the worst of the subhuman proclivities of both races. Scorpini was master executionor for the Syndicates's Chicago Midwestern Division. Malicious, cold-blooded murder was his chosen profession, and to it he applied himself with such enthusiastic zest and dedication that more than one Syndicate minion who had jumped Syndicate traces had chosen suicide rather than fall into the hands of J. Basil Scorpini.

The second of these new arrivals was Gimp Rodicco; of the same ilk as Scorpini though more sub-human if possible. Rodicco was rarely dispatched on a Syndicate job unless slaughter was involved. That was the way he liked to work, and there were very few things related to his work that he did not get exactly as he wanted. The squat, apelike Rodicco was a compulsive killer who struck like lightning and had been known to kill for no other reason than an impulsive whim.

Nick Ferroni, Bucher knew without being told, had promised both Scorpini and Rodicco millions to get them away from their established havens with the Syndicate. It could have happened no other way.

Neither Scorpini nor Rodicco even so much as glanced toward the cell where Bucher stood. Both were totally absorbed in the impending fate of Isabella, absorbed to the point of enthusiastic delight.

"You see," Yvette said, turning toward Bucher and preening proudly. "I have connections in your precious U.S. that you never even suspected. Ferroni procured them for me. They're expendable, of course, the same as Ferroni was, and will be dealt with in due time." With another mock curtsy for his benefit, she turned and strode proudly toward where Raoul and Pierre were busy tying Isabella in la Señorita de Muerte.

The instant Yvette's back was turned Bucher leaped toward the blunk where the body of Dr. Bruno von Kessler lay. He grabbed the coil of cloth torn from his undershirt and went to the side of the cell nearest the lever that activated the bolt locking the door. His moves were instinctive; the time for thinking was past, now was the time for action only. There was little chance he would not be seen by at least one of the five killers gathered around the death chair, but that was a chance he would have to take. There was no other way, period. And if he failed to lasso the lever with the circle of leather on the end of the coil on the first throw, he would never get a second chance. Of this he was certain.

His sweaty hands shook like those of a man afflicted with severe palsy as he gripped the coil and eased it through the bars, holding it for the toss. If he failed, he was dead. Bucher knew this. And so was Isabella, along with unnumbered millions who might suffer the same though by a much more horrible means within a few days—and all at the hands of a madwoman.

CHAPTER THIRTEEN

Bucher held his breath, braced himself and tossed the loop of leather made from von Kessler's belt. In spite of the effort he put forth to make the toss smoothly, it was an awkward, ungainly throw. His throat ached with tension, his tongue felt like sandpaper in his mouth, and his eyes stung from great beads of nervous perspiration that rolled down his forehead. It seemed like an eternity from the time the loop left his hand until it reached the lever—and settled silently over it, sliding down the lever to rest on the concrete floor.

Bucher's heart thudded furiously against the wall of his rib cage—like a wild animal inside trying to hammer its way to freedom. He gambled a quick look toward the chair and found all standing around it were too engrossed in the goings-on there to notice what he was doing. He inhaled deeply, took up the slack in the improvised line, and gradually, began exerting pressure. It seemed like an eternity had passed before the soft material that had been his undershirt ceased to stretch.

But at last it did, and when he pulled harder still, a keen bolt of excitement shot through him from head to toe. The lever moved an inch! Then another! Next a third, and finally a fourth. From his right, at the door of the cell, came the barely perceptible sound of metal against metal and the door, released by the bolt, relaxed outward, opening a fraction.

A shout of silent exultation gathered in Bucher's throat, though he dared not make a sound until the Walther was in his hand—then he would let it speak for him. Silent as a ghost he slipped out of the cell and around toward Ixchotl. The Indian was now on his knees and merely nodded painfully in encouragement to Bucher as he seized his silencered P-38 and a handful of loaded clips from the shelf. His switchblade fell to the floor at his feet as he did this, but Bucher ignored it. With grim expertise he checked to make certain the pistol was loaded to capacity, then strode back around to the front of the cell just as Raoul was fitting the iron collar of la Señorita Silla around Isabella's neck.

"No, no, please dear God have mercy," Isabella begged piteously—which brought a squeal of intense joy from Yvette and coarse guffaws of insane laughter from both Raoul and Pierre. Scorpini and Rodicco, standing a bit to one side, watched with huge grins of enjoyment on their brutal faces.

"Now watch her eyes bulge out as la Señorita Silla de Muerte makes love to her," Raoul shouted in high glee, hand on the large butterfly screw behind Isabella's neck. Another coarse guffaw came from his throat; the last sound he was ever to make.

"Koosh!"

The gentle death-sigh of the Walther in Bucher's big mitt was the only sound heard save Isabella's pleas, as those gathered about to watch her die saw instead a third and smaller eye appear squarely between Raoul's mad ones as Raoul shot up on his toes and was flung backward to the floor, dead before he struck it.

"The Butcher!"

This wild scream of alarm came from J. Basil Scorpini, who clawed desperately for the .38 Special under his arm. He never made it.

The Walther in Bucher's hand sighed a second time, its nine millimeter slug entering Scorpini's left eye, shattering his brain pan, and spewing fragments of bone and pinkish-grey globs of matter out the back of his skull behind him, the force of the bullet causing his body to topple to the cement floor.

Pierre, Yvette, and Rodicco fled like partridges, each in a different direction, the squat Rodicco racing with surprising speed toward the set of stairs leading upward at the end of the huge chamber opposite the tunnel. Pierre managed to make it behind a huge tier of five gallon carboys filled with water. Bucher, busy freeing Isabella, caught only a glimpse of Yvette entering the tunnel.

Sixty seconds later Bucher had Isabella free of the death chair and half-carried, half-dragged the young woman, hysterical with relief over being rescued, behind the cell, which would offer a measure of protection if fireworks broke-out.

Ixchotl stood weaving on his feet, holding onto the shelf, the wound in the man's side a gory sight to behold, though not as serious as Bucher had earlier assumed. Ixchotl's weakness was from loss of blood, and, with proper attention to the wound, he would soon be as good as new.

"That one will cause you no more trouble, Zaxatkn," he said somewhat shakily in Mayan, and not without

165

a note of pride in his voice, pointing down the chamber toward the stairs leading upward.

Gimp Rodicco lay facedown at the foot of the stairs, arms flung out crablike, the ebony shaft of Bucher's switchblade thrusting straight up out of the man's neck.

"I thank you, Ixchotl," Bucher replied in the same language. "Those stairs lead up to the old stone building that conceals the secret entrance to this place?"

"That is correct, Zaxatkn."

"How many other secret entrances and exits did Gris build?"

"Several were planned, but only one other besides that of the old stone building was completed, and only Gris knew of its location. He had the two of my people who constructed it killed to ensure its secrecy."

"Can you make it up those stairs and to a doctor by yourself, Ixchotl?"

"Now I can, yes. My weakness is gradually becoming less, and the wound is not as grave as it appears, though it is quite painful. I will be all right."

Isabella, who spoke no Mayan and who had recovered remarkably fast from her hysteria, had been looking questioningly back and forth between Bucher and Ixchotl as they talked. Suspecting Bucher was about to send her with the Indian, she shook her head vigorously when Bucher turned toward her.

"No," she pleaded in English. "Don't send me from you. I'll simply die of terror if you do."

It had been in Bucher's thoughts to send her with Ixchotl, but at her plea his decision wavered. "It can get damned hairy from here on out," he told her bleakly.

"It's been damned hairy already, Bucher. Believe

me." She shuddered. "Those creatures. They're—they're mad. Mad like we saw those poor peons in the film."

Just then Bucher remembered Dr. von Kessler's death. "Isabella, your father—"

"I know," she cut in. "That woman told me of his death just before you shot Raoul." She closed her swollen, discolored eyes, inhaled deeply to get a firm grip on herself, opened her eyes and said: "I'll make arrangements and all for poor Father later. What's next?"

"I'm going after Yvette d'Aquitaine," Bucher said grimly. She has a small notebook full of information I must have. Several hundred gallons of her MM2 are already in the states, ready to be released."

"I know. Raoul and Pierre were talking about it with those two gangsters as they held me and . . ." she looked away in shame at remembering, closing her eyes and shuddering again, ". . . as they dragged me down the tunnel."

"Can you make it up those stairs?" Bucher asked of Ixchotl in Mayan.

"Yes, with ease now," Ixchotl replied. "But you are very kind."

Bucher and Isabella walked slowly beside the Indian until they reached the corpse of Gimp Rodicco at the foot of the stone steps, waiting in silence as Ixchotl painfully mounted the stairs and passed from sight. Then Bucher knelt beside the dead man, removing from his body an Army-style, semiautomatic .45 loaded with dum-dums and a pearl-handled, nickel-plated double action 32-20.

"Which do you want?" Bucher asked Isabella.

"Both," she said grimly, small jaw clenched as fresh

tears glistened in her eyes. "I'll be forever grateful and in your debt for saving my life, Bucher," she said, fighting the tears. "But I honestly wish Raoul and those two other gangsters were not dead. Promise me something."

Bucher looked at her closely, and despite the swollen discoloration around her eyes, the bruised and puffy lips, and the blood from the wound in her temple, which had now ceased to bleed, he saw something in Isabella's face he had never seen in the face of a woman before—and hoped to never see again.

"What sort of promise?" he asked quietly.

"I want to kill Pierre." The hard, cold bitterness of her words reminded Bucher of the shattering of frozen glass. "I want to kill him because if I don't I won't ever feel clean again. I don't expect you to understand my reasons; you're not a woman, but—but . . ." She faltered, shivering, then took a mighty grip on her small self and looked Bucher straight in the eye. "They defiled me, my body, used it like a—a—I don't know what. All four of them, took turns holding me, and that woman, that creature, stood watching as—as—"

"Easy, easy." Bucher watched as she thrust the 32-20 down behind the waistband of her tattered jeans and held the .45 in her hand. "Don't think about it and it'll go away. You'll forget it in time." He could imagine the terrible ordeal she had undergone.

"I don't *want* to forget it!" she said, her voice rising. She kept pace with Bucher as he made his way toward the tier of carboys behind which Pierre had vanished. "Not until Pierre is dead, not until I kill him. Perhaps after that I can pretend it never happened, and hopefully I'll forget. But not before. Promise me, Bucher."

"Has Pierre got a gun?"

"He only believes in the garrote; he and Raoul and that woman. He claims guns are uncivilized. Do you promise?"

"I promise," Bucher told her. "Providing Pierre doesn't force me to kill him first."

Pierre was nowhere to be found behind the tier of five gallon carboys. Apparently the man had made it to the tunnel the same as Yvette.

"How long is that tunnel, and what lies beyond it?" Bucher asked Isabella in a hushed whisper as they approached the tunnel's mouth.

"It's about one hundred yards long and opens onto a large chamber like this one here, only it's man-made and not nearly as high. It's the living quarters. In it are a dozen rooms for sleeping, a living and dining area, a kitchen, a library; Gris didn't stint himself on his pocketbook. Beyond that is a large laboratory, though I only got a peek at it. But from what I saw, the equipment is modern. Raoul and Pierre are both egomaniacs; they proudly gave me the cook's tour of the place before they overpowered Gris and dragged him down the tunnel. I think they're mad."

"I know they are, and so is Yvette," Bucher said.

Isabella listened carefully as Bucher told how Yvette and her two husbands had unknowingly inhaled MM2.

"Dear God in Heaven," Isabella breathed in loathing when he finished.

"Let's get the show on the road," Bucher said. "Stay close beside me, and follow my lead in."

"Just don't you get carried away and forget your promise," Isabella gritted her teeth as she followed him into the tunnel.

169

The tunnel was poorly lit; only one small bulb every fifty feet or so, but there was sufficient light for Bucher to notice the huge drop-gate half a dozen feet inside it. The gate was constructed of narrow-gauge railroad rails welded six inches apart top and bottom on cross-pieces of the same material, the bottom of each sharpened to a point that fitted into a slot in the concrete floor when the gate was dropped.

Bucher studied the thing closely as they passed under it. It reminded him of the huge spiked gates set in the wall at the end of a drawbridge over a moat at the entrance of a medieval castle. Expect that this one was heavier, weighing several thousand pounds at least, and operated by means of a powerful electric motor instead of a windlass.

"Gris must have tapped onto San Luis Potosi's main trunk line for electricity," Bucher said quietly.

"That's right," Isabella said. "But there are also two huge motors far back in the mine that will furnish electricity if necessary. Why would Gris install a drop-gate like that?"

Bucher, searching the walls for a junction box with a switch to raise and lower the gate, did not look at her in replying.

"To prevent a surprise attack. By dropping the gate in case of attack, the enemy would be slowed long enough for Gris to escape by that exit Ixchotl said only Gris knew of. I don't see any switch to operate that big motor there. It's probably on the motor there, and well concealed, with another switch back in the living quarters more than likely, and, if I know anything at all about the criminal mind, I'll bet there's also a third switch. One located out there in the chamber we just left, perhaps around the cell, or that chair,

170

or in any one of a dozen other places. Gris would be a fool not to have a switch on both sides of the gate. Come on, let's dig those two maniacs out and get this ratrace over with." Minute by minute Bucher was growing more anxious about that small black notebook Yvette had shown him. Without that notebook he, White Hat, and the entire United States for that matter, could well be up the proverbial creek without a paddle. He looked at Isabella.

"Are you still game?"

"You better believe I'm still game—and when this is over I intend to find me a nice quiet place and cry for a week."

"Cut it out," Bucher said, not unkindly. "You're not the first woman ever to be forced."

"Damn other women!" Isabella snapped hotly. "It's the first time Isabella von Kessler has ever been forced." Her gnashing teeth sounded like two pieces of coarse sandpaper rubbing together. "Do you know the definition of gangbang—?"

"Sshhh!" Bucher stopped, motioning her to be quiet. On each side of the wide tunnel, there were numerous large pieces of mining equipment that a person could hide behind, and Bucher was certain he had heard something behind an old ore car up ahead on the right.

It turned out to be nothing—unless the noise had been made by a rat. There was no evidence of Pierre and Yvette. Nor did Bucher and Isabella find any sign of them as they neared the living quarters. They had reached these quarters and were preparing to commence a systematic search of them and the rest of the mine when the lights dimmed briefly. From behind them, at the end of the tunnel with the drop-gate, they heard the whine of a large electric motor and the dull

171

rumble of machinery. Next came the jarring thud of metal against concrete, and the motor ceased, the lights returning to full again.

"What is it, Bucher?" Isabella whispered.

"Yvette and Pierre," Bucher snarled in self-anger. "They hid in the tunnel and let us pass, then returned to the chamber where the cell is and dropped the gate. They knew where Gris' hidden switch in the chamber is located, and now they've got us caged up in here, with plenty of time for them to escape. Come on. Let's go." He broke into a fast jog with Isabella, .45 in her hand, right beside him.

Bucher's assessment of the situation was right in part. The gate was down, barring their entrance into the huge chamber, but neither Pierre nor Yvette was escaping. Pierre obviously did not want to, and Yvette could not—because Yvette was firmly ensconced in the deadly grip of la Señorita Silla de Muerte. By some path of warped reasoning known only to him, the insane Pierre had turned against the one responsible for his madness, and was now about to administer to her the same fate so many others had suffered at his hand. Yvette's arms were tied securely to the crossbar, the metal collar snug around her neck, and behind her stood Pierre, his fiendish laughter echoing a hollow death knell as it bounced off the sides of the big chamber.

"My god," Bucher rasped harshly, staring with difficulty through the bars of the cell that stood between him and the couple at the chair. "He's going to garrote Yvette."

"You said they're both mad," Isabella reminded him.

"They are both mad—but it's still a helluva way to die."

"Search for a switch to lift the gate," Isabella said hurriedly. "You said there may be one concealed around the motor somewhere. Perhaps we can save that woman. I'm not sure why we should, but I agree; it is a helluva way to die."

Though she was insane, Yvette was thoroughly conscious of her perilous predicament, her madwoman's mind telling her she teetered on the very brink of death, and in response to this her mouth opened wide, and shriek after shriek of ear-splitting, mindless terror tore from her throat to join the blood curdling laughter from Pierre.

All at once Yvette's shrieks took on a peculiar, strangled sound, and Isabella plucked the 32-20 revolver from her waistband and emptied it in measured squeezes of the trigger. The small slugs spun off the bars of the cell and ricocheted, whining around the chamber.

"Let me try." Bucher steadied his gun hand against one of the rails of the drop-gate, but did not pull the trigger. Isabella's shots had alerted Pierre to their presence, and he crouched down behind the death chair, both Yvette and the cell now protecting him from further shots from behind the gate.

Yet this new position in no way interfered with the purpose Pierre's mad brain had devised; even his hand was not visible when he reached up to the back of Yvette's neck and, between thumb and forefinger, turned the stout butterfly screw, reducing Yvette's cries of protest to ugly, grunty croaks for air. Isabella stared in frozen horror, the chilling sounds from Yvette ceasing altogether as Pierre again turned the screw.

173

She knew precisely, and all too well, the agony and terror the women seated in the chair was going through. She could still feel the impression of the cold metal collar about her own neck.

She removed her eyes from the scene at the chair to look at Bucher, who was searching furiously around the large electric motor, and when she looked back she saw Yvette's body go rigid, attempt to arch outward from the breasts down, her face turning the shade of spoiled liver as her green eyes slowly emerged from their sockets and her tongue crept straight and far out from between lips oddly contorted in a grimace of death. She maintained this gruesome position for perhaps fifteen seconds, then collapsed like an inner tube with a bad leak.

"Stand clear!" Bucher rasped. "I found it!" The large toggle switch had been cleverly hidden beneath a large glob of hard wax. Isabella obeyed, and the big drop-gate was less than waist high when she and Bucher scrambled under it.

"No!" Isabella's voice lashed the big chamber as Bucher headed at a run for the chair. "She's dead, Bucher. Nothing can save her now. And you made me a promise. Stand aside, and don't interfere."

Bucher halted in mid-stride and turned to face the small, thoroughly feminine young woman he had known little more than twenty-four hours and, paradoxically, in that peculiar way the human mind is sometimes known to function, fragments of their togetherness in the Land Rover the night before flickered across his memory. In a twinkling he recalled her tender insistence, her gentle greediness as they lay there surrounded by the vast hush of the Mexican wilderness, the softness of her lips against his, and, inexplicably, these recollections were followed immediately by imaginary scenes of her desperate struggles against the brutal mass assaults from Raoul, Pierre, Scorpini, and Rodicci.

"That's right, Isabella," he said quietly. "I made you a promise, and I'm keeping it. Go ahead and kill the sonofabitch, and take all the time you want doing it."

What difference did it make whether he or Isabella, or someone else, killed Pierre. Insane or not, the sonofabitch had no right to live, and besides, Bucher knew instinctively nobody was going to take Pierre alive. The man was an aggressive, homicidal maniac who must be killed to be stopped.

This assessment of Pierre was confirmed when the man sidled catlike from behind the death chair, Bucher's switchblade, which Pierre had taken from Gimp Rodicco's body, glittering evilly in his hand. Bucher shucked his heater, just in case, when Pierre dropped into a wide-legged half-squat, flicking the knife back and forth from hand to hand too fast for the eye to follow, in the ancient Korean style of close-quarters combat with a knife. Bucher soon saw his precaution of drawing his gun was unnecessary. Isabella, .45 in her small hand, never batted an eye nor retreated a step as Pierre crept closer.

The Army-style, semiautomatic .45 in Isabella's hand was loaded with eight deadly dum-dums. The gun had been especially designed to stop Moro tribesmen insane on hemp before one of them could lop half a dozen innocent heads with a bolo. The weapon had far exceeded all expectations of performance. The relatively slow speed of the big slug not only stopped a tribesman cold if it hit him dead center, it sent him

175

sprawling if it so much as hit a finger. Bucher, recalling Isabella's expertise with the snub-nosed .38 in the Diablo, suspected she was familiar with the capabilities of the weapon she held on Pierre at present.

Mentally Bucher shrugged indifference. Whether he approved or appreciated what he was about to witness was entirely beside the point. It was just one of those things that had to be. If Isabella did not down the man, then Bucher would have to do so and, quite honestly, he saw no means of doing so without a gun. Again, and now more obviously than ever, Pierre did not intend to be taken alive. Personally Bucher would have felt no remorse if the man were fed alive into a meat grinder. Pierre did not deserve to live, had forfeited his place in the human race when he raped the young woman who now faced him, to say nothing of his murdering Gris, Rojas, Yvette, and God alone knew how many others.

A softly sibilant, evil chuckle issued from Pierre's throat. A rope of slobber drooled from his chin to the floor, and a small pocket of froth was gathered at each corner of his mouth. He was only a short distance from the chair when he forsook his half-squat stance and streaked toward Isabella, switchblade at the ready, the huge chamber filled to the ceiling with his fiendish howl.

Isabella made no move for a long beat-three, stood as if waiting for some signal from a director. Pierre was ten yards away when her hand whipped up.

"Barrroom!" Heavy forty-five caliber thunder bludgeoned the chamber mightily. The 255 grain lubaloy slug loafing along at a comparatively slow 860 feet per second, and the walloping mule-kick power of 500 pounds struck Pierre equidistant between elbow and

shoulder joint. The force of his headlong charge combined with the sledgehammer force of the slug blasting through his arm practically tore the arm off and slammed him into the air, pinwheeling him as one might sail an empty pie tin. He landed face down and spread-eagled, all except his shattered left arm, which lay across the back of his neck.

Perhaps in his madness he feels no pain, Bucher thought in grim silence as Pierre scrambled with amazing speed to his feet.

Pierre still held the switchblade in his hand, and this time was much closer to Isabella. Again she did not retreat when he lunged at her.

"Barrroom!"

Due to the forward angle of Pierre's lunging body, this second slug struck parallel to his backbone at the top of the left buttock, ripped a gory hole through this fleshy section of his anatomy, exited from his body and entered it again, this time striking the back of his heel and lodging among the fine bones of his instep. The pile-driving force of the slug drove him to the floor again, this time to his side, and also penetrated the blood-lust of his madness sufficiently to inform him of what had occurred thus far and what was likely to occur in the immediate future. The enraged cry of a mortally wounded beast sprang from his mouth, now more slobbery and more frothy than ever. He was covered with his own blood; it spewed from his body in three places.

Clumsily, awkwardly, the man scrambled up to stand on his one good foot, putting distance between himself and Isabella in the process. He was twenty yards from her, balancing himself on one foot, eyes darting back and forth between Bucher and Isabella

177

and strangely, as he spoke, Bucher saw that the man's eyes were totally devoid of the madness that had filled them earlier.

"You're trying to kill me!" he snarled indignantly in clear, concise English.

"You raped me!" Isabella spat in return. From where he stood a couple of steps to one side, Bucher could almost feel the physical heat of her anger.

Pierre glared at her in virulent hatred for half a minute, fingering the knife still held in his good hand, then a dirty sneer warped his handsome features. "And you were a lousy go, bitch. What do you want from me? Two dollars?" Almost too quick for the eye to catch, he flipped the knife, caught the tip with the practiced ease of a knife-throwing artist, and whipped his arm back over his head.

"Barrroom! Barrroom! Barrroom!"

The .45's triple blast of thunder seemed to rock the chamber, the sound still reverberating against the walls as Pierre was hurled up and back off his foot, landing in an ugly, ungainly heap half a dozen feet from where he had been standing. This time he did not scramble up. Nor did he ever move again.

Isabella dropped the gun and stood perfectly motionless for a long minute, looking at the man she had killed, without expression. Then she walked with wooden gait to 'the cell and entered to stand looking down at her dead father. Once she bent low over the old man, softly whispered something Bucher was unable to hear, then left the cell, and with the same awkward gait made her way to the foot of the stairs where the corpse of Gimp Rodicco lay. Slowly she mounted the stairs, stiffly and at one step at the time, stopping to wait for Bucher when she reached the top.

Bucher's first move was to secure the small notebook from Yvette, which he managed to do without looking at the grisly caricature of horror that so recently had been a woman of breathtaking beauty. He turned through the notebook until he was satisfied it contained the information Yvette had told him about, information that would enable White Hat to locate and destroy all the MM2 stashed in the United States, then he placed the notebook safely in an inside coat pocket and stood looking listlessly at the carnage about him.

Five men dead, one woman dead, all dead because of greed for gold, of lust for power, of unmitigated human sonofabitchery.

I wonder when the slaughter is going to stop, he asked himself bleakly, a tired slump coming to his big shoulders. Then he turned and walked wearily toward the stairs where Isabella waited, the bitter-sour taste of defeat strong in his mouth.

the Executioner

Violence is a man! His name is Edge...

The bloodiest action-series ever published, with a hero who is the meanest, most vicious killer the West has ever seen.

It's sharp —
It's hard —
It's EDGE

GEORGE G. GILMAN

Order		Title	Book #	Price
_____	# 1	THE LONER	P109	.95¢
_____	# 2	TEN GRAND	P115	.95¢
_____	# 3	APACHE DEATH	P133	.95¢
_____	# 4	KILLER'S BREED	P148	.95¢
_____	# 5	BLOOD ON SILVER	P172	.95¢
_____	# 6	RED RIVER	P190	.95¢
_____	# 7	CALIFORNIA KILL	P221	.95¢
_____	# 8	HELL'S SEVEN	P265	.95¢
_____	# 9	BLOODY SUMMER	P293	.95¢
_____	#10	BLACK VENGEANCE	P333	.95¢
_____	#11	SIOUX UPRISING	P360	.95¢

AND MORE TO COME . . .

TO ORDER

Please check the space next to the book s you want, send this order form together with your check or money order, include the price of the book/s and 25¢ for handling and mailing to:

PINNACLE BOOKS, INC.   P.O. Box 4347
Grand Central Station / New York, N.Y. 10017

☐ **CHECK HERE IF YOU WANT A FREE CATALOG**

I have enclosed $_____check_____or money order_____
as payment in full. No C.O.D.'s

Name_____

Address_____

City_____State_____Zip_____
(Please allow time for delivery)